MANTRA-6
BRIMSTONE

RUSSEL HUTCHINGS

Dedication

This book is dedicated to the men of the SAS Regiment
– Both Past and Present -

To my wife Nunik and my children.

Acknowledgements

To my sister Alana for her belief in me and her unwavering support and assistance in getting this novel to print.

To Vince Long for his tireless efforts and encouragement.

To Adrian d'Hage for his invaluable help and guidance that was most generously given.

To Graham Brammer for taking the time to guide me in the early stages of writing this novel.

The SAS Warrior

Fate whispered to the SAS Warrior...

'You cannot withstand the storm'

The SAS Warrior whispered back to fate...

'I am the Storm'

Chapter 1

'The Abyss'

THAI-CAMBODIA BORDER
1990

The hum of the MC-130 TALON Special Operations aircraft seemed louder than usual. John Devereaux's senses were on heightened alert, elevating his sensitivity to that and those around him. He had exited aircraft such as this over 800 times, but always as part of a team. On this moonless night, his lonely step into the abyss was only the start of a mission that would test him to his very core, both professionally and personally. No team for support; no one to rely on, he was alone.

When he left the ramp of the C-130, he was a NOC - a non-official cover operative seconded to the Australian

1

Secret Intelligence Service (ASIS) to do their dirty work. A man forged in the SAS - his mission had begun.

The Loadmaster raised his hand, showing a three-fingered hand signal.

'Three minutes.'

Turning away and clearing his oxygen hose to avoid standing on it, the Loadmaster leaned against the inner fuselage to stabilise himself on the ramp and watched as the unknown high-altitude-high-opening (HAHO) jumper prepared himself.

The Loadmaster was a big man at 190 centimetres but looked docile for someone that size. He gazed over at Devereaux, having never met him or seen his face before.

When Devereaux boarded the TALON, his face was already covered with a lightweight woollen black balaclava. To the aircraft crew, he was an enigma – a package they knew better than to ask questions about. Their only role was to deliver the package.

The Loadmaster looked over at Devereaux, and

as they made eye contact, the Loadmaster shook his head as if to say, 'you crazy bastard'. Devereaux gave a slight grin, indicated only through his wincing eyes behind his clear helmet visor, and then continued his final checks.

Devereaux felt the pressure change in his ears as the aircraft started to depressurise. Partway down the fuselage was a thick black curtain that blocked off the rear of the plane.

This area was the blackout area, where the only light used was a dull-red ambient light designed to assist in maintaining night vision and to reduce visibility from the ground. All windows of the TALON were blacked out. To the rear of the heavy curtain was a restricted area – the curtain-shrouded a small two-man capsule that housed highly sensitive electronic warfare equipment. The equipment was used by SpecOps to jam enemy communication systems or to listen to radio chatter that could impact the operation.

This is what made the TALON a potent aircraft for infiltrating into enemy-held territory. Painted entirely in matt black, something was very menacing and indeed sinister about a TALON.

The red 'jump' light was now illuminated. Devereaux moved to the central oxygen console and disconnected his oxygen hose through which he had spent the last hour pre-breathing.

He connected his two-bailout bottles, which would provide him with another 30 minutes of oxygen – enough for his journey into the abyss.

Making one final check of his equipment and ensuring his prototype helmet-mounted night vision goggles (NVG's) were locked into place, he looked over at the Loadmaster and gave a thumbs-up signal. He was good to go.

The Loadmaster raised his index finger, 'One minute!'

The rear door and ramp opened into position revealing a black hole through which no light seemed to penetrate.

Devereaux looked for some visible feature, but it was just a canvas of black.

He peered into the black void beyond the edge of the jump ramp, willing himself to keep his heart rate under control.

The Loadmaster crossed his fingers and shouted, 'Thirty seconds!'

Devereaux moved to the edge of the ramp aided by the Loadmaster, his equipment tormenting his body and his movement. Finally, he turned around and faced back into the aircraft. He edged his way backwards until he was balancing on the balls of his feet; his heels just over the edge of the ramp as if to tease the darkness - he was ready!

Devereaux ignored the weight of his equipment that made this form of infiltration agonisingly painful on the body, at least in the early stages, before exiting the aircraft. Outside, of course, everything would become relatively weightless, no longer supported by muscle and stressed joints.

Glancing at his altimetres, he noticed the needles breaching 37,000 feet. Shit, it's cold, he thought. Even though his gloves, he could feel the icy air. However, he knew this would all change as he entered the tropical layers. The air warmed up with every thousand feet he descended; soon, he would be sweating like a pig as the humidity and ground temperature kicked in.

For a moment, Devereaux reflected on what lay ahead of him.

He glanced over his left shoulder at the jump lights and the Loadmaster and awaited the void that beckoned him.

Green lights pierced the immediate ramp area, and the Loadmaster pointed outside into the night as Devereaux stepped backwards and exited the aircraft.

The slipstream hit him in the chest at 190-knots. For an instant, it felt like being smacked in the chest by a cricket bat.

Maintain the exit position...

Rotate on aircraft heading...

Stabilise and monitors altimetres...

Devereaux goes through the drill.

Speed accelerating...

Stability fine...

The TALON's silhouette rapidly disappeared into the night sky.

Devereaux was on his way, breaching the border undetected. Given the altitude and the commercial airline route being taken, the aircraft would not be heard from the ground due to the two layers of cloud the sound would have to pass through.

'Heading fine, altitude 31,800'.

Passing through the first layer of cloud, Devereaux thought how eerie this place was. No visible object in sight, just the dim glow from his altimetres was the only visible sign. At 26,700', Devereaux prepared to deploy the main chute, the MT1-XX, Tactical Glide Parachute System, a 360sq foot canopy most commonly used by Special Ops Teams for standoff operations such as this. At 25,000', Devereaux had calculated a glide capacity of 15.1kms – 5km more than required for the insertion. Devereaux continued to eyeball the altimeter and released the ripcord as the needle struck 26,000'. The canopy opening was controlled, taking a little longer to deploy than usual thanks to the extra stows, he put into the parachute suspension lines, as well as the additional fold to the canopy.

This slower opening ensured that there was no great jolt on deployment, making it a less stressful one on the equipment, and, of course, on himself.

The canopy deployed correctly and was fixed on half breaks, reducing its forward speed and allowing Devereaux time to prepare for further flight.

Reaching down and manoeuvring his hands through tight crevasses between his equipment, he adjusted his harness to get a better sitting position for the long descent ahead.

He then reached down to open his NAV Console to reveal a GPS, which had the flight plan already pre-programmed in it. Next to the GPS was a compass, a digital altimeter, and a mild illumination cell to provide visuals on the Console. Devereaux mentally ticked off his checklist: 'track required 095°, altitude 24,000' - the programme is active'.

'Course set to Landing Zone (LZ) - Cambodia!' he said to himself.

Turning on course to match that of the GPS, Devereaux eased up on the toggles located behind the parachute risers to allow the canopy to generate more lift and speed.

This gave him more coverage across the ground beneath him and ensuring maximum penetration across the border into Cambodia, his ultimate landing zone.

At 18,000', the second layer of cloud engulfed him.

As he entered the clouds, he eased up on the toggles once again, and the canopy began to get buffeted by the colliding air temperatures that caused the turbulence. Pulling down on his toggle into the half brake position, he had hoped that would sort the turbulence out. However, the turbulence grew stronger, so he eased up once again only to be rocked violently from side to side.

He looked up as he was again hit by intense buffeting and saw the right-hand side of his canopy had collapsed. He started to spiral rapidly to the right. Instantly, he tried to counter the spiral by pulling hard on the left steering toggle, hoping to re-inflate the collapsed cells - however, the spinning became more violent as the turbulence became stronger. Devereaux looked down to locate the cut-away handle in case he needed to deploy the reserve parachute.

'Not yet' he thought.

Looking down at his altimeters, he had lost over 2,000 feet, and that was increasing. Devereaux looked up at the canopy once again and saw that the right side was like a limp bed sheet flapping in the wind.

If he couldn't clear it in the next few seconds, he would have to cut-away, or he would not be able to reach the landing zone. That wasn't an option he wanted to take just yet.

He was rapidly descending and was rotating to the point of going out of control.

He was falling into an abyss, total darkness all around him, his rate of descent increasing, - his heart pounding harder! Devereaux reached up high on the rear risers and pulled them both down bringing the canopy into a stall position and then quickly released them allowing the canopy to rush forward, forcing air back into the cells.

It worked, all cells were now fully inflated, and he was flying once again. He had lost 3,000 feet, and his heart was pounding, but he knew he had to calm himself and get back to work.

He took a deep breath and breathed out slowly and then repeated the process once again... He was back on task!

Devereaux maintained intense concentration as he checked his altitude and bearing.

He made some adjustments to his heading and brought the canopy back on course.

'Altitude is lower than needed for the glide slope to LZ' he thought.

Adjusting for the required glide slope, Devereaux eased the steering toggles up into the full flight position, allowing the canopy to gain lift, and to maintain a better attitude to meet the needs of the required glide slope to the LZ.

Breaking out of the cloud base at 16,500', Devereaux could make out scattered lights emanating from distant villages surrounding the Khmer town of Pailin. Lights from vehicles travelling along far off roads could be seen. The ground he was flying across, however, stood black as a raven. Bearing and glideslope on track as Devereaux eased up on the steering toggles and allowed the canopy to fly at full speed once again.

At 12,000', Devereaux reached up and released one side of his oxygen mask, no longer needing O2. The instant relief he experienced was a welcome feeling as the equipment was uncomfortable at best, especially considering the tropical humidity surrounding him – a sensation made even warmer due to the thermal clothing, he had needed to wear for insertion from 37,000'.

The needles of the altimeters now showed 6,000'.

He reached up to his helmet.

Night vision down, in place and active.

Adjust focus.

'Let there be light', Devereaux thought to himself.

Devereaux scanned his GPS and altimeter before looking for matching terrain indicators to confirm LZ proximity. He identified the LZ, 10° right of the current track. He adjusted his course and commenced his approach to the LZ – a padi field and welcomed return to terra firma. 1,500ft... Devereaux reached down and released the equipment straps and lowered his combat equipment onto his feet.

Wind check. He was making a downwind approach to the LZ.

1,000ft... Devereaux scanned the area and picked his landing point and commenced a turn to the left to enter the base leg of his approach. One more turn and he was into finals.

Devereaux executed the final left turn into the wind and stabilised the canopy. 30ft...

Pointing his toes down, Devereaux allowed his combat equipment to be lowered on a suspension rope, which now dangled two meters below his feet.

The ground rushed by underneath as he brought the canopy into a gentle flare, washing off most of the forward speed.

His equipment came in contact with the ground, followed by his feet.

He immediately pulled hard on the right toggle to help collapse the canopy and went straight to ground to minimise his silhouette.

Lying flat on the ground, Devereaux removed his harness, freeing himself of constraints, and readied his Heckler & Koch MP5-SD suppressed submachine gun. He then removed his helmet, listening and looking carefully for any signs of movement.

'All good', he muttered to himself. He quickly commenced stowing the parachute and its rigging into a parachute valise. Gathering his equipment, he moved 100m to the south, where the rainforest started. After moving into the forest another 100m, he found a suitable site to bury his parachute equipment.

Devereaux buried all non-essential equipment to lighten his load and allow him to move faster. Using a small shovel, he dug a hole and carefully placed the equipment inside.

He removed a glass bottle containing a clear fluid. Careful to cover his nose and mouth to avoid the noxious vapours, he poured the solution generously over the equipment. Devereaux could hear the chemical working instantly – a steady hiss as it went to work. He started filling in the hole, pausing from time to time to listen for anything that might be approaching his position. Finally, he camouflaged the site and moved back to the edge of the jungle and padi field.

CHAPTER 2

'The Asset'

DFAT-ASIS Ops Room
Canberra, 0800hrs

Director-General Fletcher Stevens and Deputy Director Magnus Webb walked along the passageway and then turned into a stairwell. They descended the stairs to the basement level and walked along a corridor towards two glass doors. As they approached the door, Stevens swiped his key card across the scanner, and the two entered into the ASIS Operations Centre. As they passed by the rows of desks and computers, Webb looked about and saw the various ops teams and analysts busy at work managing operations around the globe. Webb opened a heavy wooden door that led into a room where live ops could be watched in real-time. On the walls, several large monitors, on the desks, computer systems with their screens glowing a soft light in the darkened environment.

'OK, listen up people, if you are not directly working on DG Steven's project, clear the room now thank you.' Webb ordered.

All but two people stood and left the room.

'Good evening Myra' said Stevens as he handed her a document.

'Put the geo-sync up on screen one please' he asked.

Myra, a 28-year-old analyst from Sydney, looked at the document briefly, taking in the pertinent information and started to bring up satellite imagery in real-time.

'Just a minute sir, we are coming online… right about now.' She said as the screen flickered, and the image came into focus.

The picture was grainy and somewhat challenging to make out any real detail.

'Can you clean that up? Asked Webb.

'On to it already, Sir, there is a little interference as there is a thin layer of cloud covering the target area. But we should get some better vision in a few minutes as it looks like it is clearing' Myra said. Stevens stood watching the screen, his right arm across his stomach, the other arm tucked into his chest, with his hand gently tucked under

15

his chin, as he waited for the image to clear. Webb looked over at Dan, who was an operations management specialist.

'Dan, what's the latest?'

'Morning Sir, the latest we have is that the Asset left the ramp of the Talon at 05:00hrs "KILO" time, that's 02:00hrs local time Cambodia. As far as we know, there was no hiccup with delivering the Asset. Now it's a waiting game sir until his next scheduled contact, which is about 24hrs or so from now.'

'Thanks, Dan, keep me updated of any changes' said Webb.

The image on the screen was now reasonably clear, but the satellite would pass in a few minutes, giving them little time to observe the target area. However, they were able to see the terrain and the immediate area in which Devereaux would be working in. The town of Pailin to the north of the target area stood out very well indeed with city lights glistening through the break-in cloud cover. Intermittently they were able to make out the road that led to the farmhouse, and to the villages further along the way. The padi fields contrasted against the hills, dense jungle, and the winding river that designated the Thai-Cambodian border.

'Myra, can you zoom in on sector "Charlie-Three" please?' asked Stevens.

The image began to get larger and larger until the target area, a farmhouse, had almost filled the screen. The image a little grainy due to the magnification, but workable. In the surrounding area and to the side of the farmhouse was a truck and in front of that truck, were what looked to be people standing in two lines. Stevens stood a little closer, concentrating on the screen.

He raised his hand up and pointed to the left-hand bottom of the screen and then turned to Myra.

'Myra, is that people standing near the truck? It looks like soldiers lined up in ranks' Stevens asked.

'Soldiers by the look of it, Sir, two ranks of ten men and three off to the side.'

'Twenty-three soldiers' thought Stevens. He turned to Magnus and said...

'Well, the Asset better have his shit squared away ol' mate, as he certainly wasn't briefed on such a force being on the ground. Our local intel said no more than six.'

Magnus Webb stepped closer to the screen and looked intently at the ranks of soldiers before the screen started to flicker and get grainier.

'What's wrong with the feed?' asked Webb.

17

'We are losing satellite coverage – ok, we're now offline… sorry, Sir.' Myra replied.

Webb turned back to Stevens, a stern look on his face.

'Well, that does create somewhat of a predicament, but the Asset is highly trained, and I am sure he will assess the situation and make the most appropriate call.'

Stevens and Webb walk back out of the Ops Room and back upstairs to the DG's office. Sitting behind his desk, Stevens turned a pen from tip to tip as a myriad of thoughts raced through his head. Sitting in front of him on a cream sofa, Webb sat in silence, as he too was pondering the troop levels on the ground.

'I personally briefed him of the importance of this mission and its ramifications for the future UNTAC mission into Cambodia. I just hope he doesn't think his skin is more valuable than the desired outcome and abort the mission.' Stevens said coldly.

Webb, sitting with his legs crossed, both arms stretched out along the backrest of the sofa, looked back over to Stevens.

'Well that's mighty-mercenary of you Fletcher' said Webb. 'I am quite sure he will complete the task as assigned,' he added.

The room was quiet for a brief moment, then Stevens left his chair and walked over to the window and peered out.

'Yes, you are quite right - I am sure he will,' came a voice, with an air of more confidence. 'My main concern Magnus is that if this all goes balls up, we will be left embarrassed in the press once again. After the Sheraton Hotel cock-up in Melbourne, we can hardly benefit from such additional exposure.'

'I must say though; I was surprised with the number of troops on target. Devereaux is going to be quite annoyed that the intel was so wrong concerning the enemy disposition.' Webb said.

'Well, that's the nature of intelligence isn't it Magnus? Intelligence is fluid, what is correct "NOW" may not be in 24 hours. It's something we all need to deal with, and Devereaux, as well as us, need to keep that in mind.'

'Yes, I'm sure he will be. Nevertheless, he is up to the task so let's see how it unfolds.

CHAPTER 3

'Once More into The Fray'

CAMBODIA

Devereaux, dressed in dark denim trousers and an olive coloured work shirt, his clothes had no identifiable markings – all tags had been removed during the sterilisation phase before infiltration.

Even his weapons had their serial numbers ground off to avoid any possibility of tracing them back to the source of origin.

Sweat poured from Devereaux's forehead; the humidity in the jungle was relentless. His clothes were starting to saturate with sweat, and he knew he had to maintain his water intake or suffer the consequences of dehydration, something unforgiving in this environment.

He was truly alone and needed all of his wits to complete the assignment.

Devereaux reflected on the briefing that ASIS Director-General Stevens had given him on the 5th floor of the Department of Foreign Affairs and Trade (DFAT) building in Canberra.

It was as though Stevens delivered the mission on a silver platter – an assignment Devereaux was made for. The mission was a target interdiction task to terminate General Pim, a Khmer Rouge (KR) Commander and Financial Controller. The second target was General Sompon Getti of the Thai Special Forces. Getti had gone rogue in favour of running his own private little war in the shadows.

Stevens stood at 180cm, red-haired, slightly balding and with a weathered face. Devereaux recalled that Stevens had put on some weight since he last saw him, a by-product of no longer being a field operative. Stevens' voice, however, was commanding and his green eyes were piercing.

'The purpose of this interdiction mission is to neutralise any possible developments or obstacles to the United Nations Transitional Authority in Cambodia (UNTAC) by strangling the financial and logistical capacity of KR remnants. This will help to pave the way for

Australia's involvement and ultimate command of the UNTAC mission, scheduled for January 1992' Stevens stated.

Stevens made it clear this mission was 'Operationally Deniable,' an off-the-books operation run by ASIS, who needed to level the playing field before UNTAC commenced its mission.

However, black-bag operations, such as this, were no longer sanctioned or within the scope of the ASIS charter. Devereaux was their instrument by which they could achieve the desired outcome. As their Non-Official Cover (NOC) operative, Devereaux would be given no support once on the ground and over the border. More importantly, he would be disavowed if he were to be caught.

Stevens passed a large manila file to Devereaux. Red stripes adorned the edges with 'Top Secret' at the header and footer along with an acronym that was in a large font and read: 'AUSTEO' (Australian Eyes Only) just beneath it. Page one was all about General Dang Pim. He was once the commander of a two thousand plus Khmer Rouge guerrilla force.

Pim's forces over the last four years had dwindled and now numbered less than 300. Nevertheless, he commanded a small, but very effective, force – mainly criminal-based operations rather than military endeavours. Pim's activities were primarily in the western regions of Cambodia, with its centre of influence in the Pailin area along the Thai-Cambodian border. His militia was disbursed, as would be expected from a guerrilla force. It was in control of the gem and illegal logging trade along Cambodia's western border with Thailand.

This fact had allowed Pim to finance current and future operations to destabilise the ruling government, with the ultimate aim of resurrecting the Khmer Rouge and ousting the government from power.

He reported directly to Pol Pot, who still wielded considerable influence and commanded pockets of resistance through commanders like Pim in Cambodia's west and south.

Reading on, Devereaux was astounded that even though Saloth Sar (Pol Pot's birth name) was 67 years of age and had been defeated by the Vietnamese Army in 1979, he maintained influence over many of his former commanders.

His sanctuary on Thai soil was an aggravation tolerated by many foreign countries after his murderous reign between 1975 and 1979, where close to two million Cambodians were murdered.

Pim had remained loyal to Pol Pot since the defeat, although Pim's ideology had transcended that of the 1975 KR doctrine.

The dossier concluded that Pim was receiving clandestine support from a rogue Thai General, Sompon Getti, who, in return for his help, received precious gems and profited enormously from Cambodia's prosperous illegal timber trade. Gen. Getti's support included the supply of weapons, ammunition and equipment as well as turning a blind eye to the Khmer Rouge's frequent cross border incursions to seek haven.

'Devereaux', Stevens said, 'General Getti is a Special Forces commander based at Camp Erawan in Lop Buri in central Thailand. He is in his mid 60's and now commands Special Forces elements along Thailand's eastern borders with Cambodia.

He has amassed a fortune over the past five years through illegal activities with no concerns as to the people or areas that his efforts ultimately destroyed. In essence, he's running his own dirty little war and maintaining instability along Thailand's border to help mask his private operations.'

Devereaux recalled Steven's monotonous voice as he delivered the mission statement: 'your mission, Devereaux, is to terminate both Pim and Getti at a

24

scheduled meeting to be held at a small farmhouse 9kms Southeast of Pailin.

ASIS assets have provided intelligence that the meeting will take place at 0900hrs, 48 hours from now. The Intel provided also indicated that Pim and Getti would arrive together, in the same vehicle, to meet subordinate field commanders to discuss future operations', Stevens added.

The location for the meeting was 1.5km from Devereaux's current position so most of Devereaux's initial movement would be across padi fields backing on to the jungle and high ground.

He knew that if compromised en route to the target area, he would push into the jungle and disappear, however, he needed to be in position before first light to set up an observation post (OP) to surveil the killing area and all approaches to and from the area.

Pim had used the farmhouse several times over the past 12 months – a fact that would prove to be his undoing.

As dawn was approaching, the jungle came to life. The noise of animals and insects became louder, making it very difficult to hear anyone approaching. As dawn broke, Devereaux was in a position overlooking the farmhouse. He saw no sign of movement.

Devereaux set about making a hide and firing position where he could lay in wait undetected. He would be on target for the next 24 hours, so he had to ensure his position was both comfortable and functional. It had to allow for minimal movement, as he would eat, drink, piss and shit in the one location. Discipline − immense discipline − would be needed.

His hide provided excellent observation of the farmhouse and surrounding area, which was mainly, cultivated land used for rice and various fruit growing.

He positioned himself so that he had depth from view so that even after the shot was taken, there would be no sign of the firing position. Devereaux made sure that the hide had two escape routes − one to the south, which skirted a bamboo cluster and was rather dark even in the daytime. Another escape route led off to the north-west contouring a ridgeline − again providing outstanding cover and quick movement away from the hide location.

Devereaux's main concern was directly behind him. The primary jungle and climbing in elevation.

His concern was that he would not have adequate warning of anyone approaching as they roamed the forest.

Nevertheless, it did have good cover from the rear as the secondary rainforest was thicker in the area, and that provided him with some comfort that he wouldn't be seen. His departure from the hide, via one of the two selected escape routes, provided excellent cover from view and from fire.

Devereaux set up and placed his Heckler & Koch PSG-1 Sniper rifle in position. The PSG-1 had long been Devereaux's weapon of choice for short-range Interdiction Missions such as this. The 7.62mm projectile was perfect for tropical conditions and heavy enough to punch through light-skinned vehicles and foliage.

0800hrs

Looking in the distance, Devereaux could see a road junction that was lined with sparse trees.

'Range it', he thought to himself.

Placing the eyepiece of the laser range finder up to his eye, he put the vertical line on the display parallel to match that of the road. He ensured the target radicle was fixed onto the junction and then depressed the rubber button on top of the range finder. The display function showed "SCAN", with three small dashes flashing off and on. Within seconds the range was tabulated, and the three flashing dashes turned into solid digits. The scan indicated a distance of 934m - just short of the junction.

27

Above the range indicator was the bearing to the junction. Devereaux marked the range and bearing on his range card, which provided him with the key features and ranges to objects around his chosen killing ground. The farmhouse, the parking area outside the farmhouse, the padi field shade hut along the main access road, the coconut tree cluster, the wind direction at the time of last entry indicated by an arrow marked in a blue China-Graph pencil - everything was registered on the range card; no detail was left untouched.

Devereaux stopped what he was doing and listened intently for any unnatural sounds, such as human movement, letting his ears pick up on anything behind him. After 30 seconds, the only sounds he could hear were the sounds of the jungle.

Devereaux got back on target, monitoring everything in the killing area and surrounding environment, looking for places of possible cover that an enemy might take.

He searched for possible escape routes, and for any dead ground where he might not be able to see an enemy hiding once the shit hit the fan. Every minute was utilised to gain atmospherics – the process of soaking up his environment, to know everything there was about it. In the distance, a noise infiltrated the natural surrounds. A small 2-Stroke motorcycle approached from the east and turned right at the junction and onto a dirt track, headed towards the farmhouse.

Looking through his Carl Zeiss 25x50 scope, Devereaux identified a lone rider wearing dark blue clothing reminiscent of early period KR, a red and white checked scarf, was draped around the rider's neck, but no weapon was seen.

A black baseball cap adorned the head of the rider, a girl in her late teens or early 20s, he thought. Her long black hair was worn in a ponytail that blew in the breeze as she closed in on the farmhouse. The old two-stroke Honda she was riding billowed a dark-grey smoke from its exhaust as she approached.

Stopping at the front of the dwelling, she placed the bike stand down, hopped off of the motorcycle and went inside, leaving the bike running.

'Range it,' he thought.

It was 518m – that was the distance he'd have to shoot tomorrow, cold bore. It was well within the effective range of the PSG-1 in such conditions. He would need all his skill to make just two rapid shots dispatching both Pim and Getti – any more than that, and he risked giving away his position.

After only five minutes, the rider exited the farmhouse and left on her motorcycle the same way she had come.

29

No other sign of life was seen. What could she possibly have been doing in there? Devereaux thought.

The day was spent developing and improving his hide as well as observing the killing area and approaches.

Devereaux adjusted and further prepared his firing position so that he could produce the most favourable shot. His range card was updated continuously, and his role now was to wait and observe.

1900hrs

The night was falling, and within 30 minutes, it would be pitch black. Little, if any moonlight would provide illumination and clouds had formed late in the afternoon, dousing the area in heavy rain.

The jungle was alive with noises; it was a place that Devereaux had, over many years, become familiar and comfortable with. In the distance, lights flickered; no doubt from other houses some way off.

Suddenly, a light emanated from a room in the farmhouse. There had been no movement all day, and now there was a sign of life?

Who is in the house? Devereaux thought.

His NVGs, at this range, would be useless, but the scope on his PSG-1 would, to some degree, allow him to see movement through the window. Was it a lone figure, or were there more people inside? Then, as quickly as the light came into existence, it shut off.

Who was that and why haven't I seen them all day? Devereaux's mind raced with possibilities.

0800hrs

Devereaux managed to catch small amounts of sleep throughout the night, but never more than 30 minutes at a time. He had recommenced observation at 0400hrs and had prepared everything for the crux that lay ahead.

Devereaux set up a small Satellite Communications (SATCOM) system and keyed in a five-letter crack code 'QTNVE'. If Devereaux were to press the send button, the crack code would be sent, indicating the mission completed.

This would allow Devereaux to remain undetected electronically as the transmission would be a burst transmission that would be sent in a millisecond, leaving no real traceable signature.

Scanning the area, he noticed the same motorcycle seen the day before coming along the dirt road leading to the farmhouse. The same girl parked her bike at the side of the building then entered it, carrying containers of what looked like food. A few minutes later, a man in a green military KR uniform exited the farmhouse carrying an AK-47 over his shoulder and ate a banana before discarding the skin by the parked motorcycle.

So, there you are. How many of you are there? Devereaux thought.

0850hrs

Everything was ready, and Devereaux was waiting for his targets to arrive before delivering the fatal shots.

Range checked.

Wind zero.

Slightly overcast skies.

He was ready!

0903hrs

A small Toyota Hi-Lux approached the farmhouse with four armed men in the back, one with an RPG.

As the Hi-Lux arrived at the farmhouse, the four-armed men dismounted and met by seven other soldiers who exited the farmhouse.

Shit, this just keeps getting better, Devereaux thought.

Looking through the scope, he noticed that the men were scurrying around and forming into a single rank. He lifted the crosshairs off the men and onto the dirt road and saw a white sedan approaching.

This is it, he thought. The rifle butt fit snugly into his shoulder.

Devereaux scanned and tracked the vehicle as it approached.

It came to a halt as a soldier raced to open the door. Devereaux noted that there was only the driver and one passenger in the vehicle... Pim!

But there was no sign of Getti.

What the fuck? Devereaux thought.

Crosshairs on target, safety-catch to fire, breathing settles, trigger pressure taken up.

Where the hell is Getti? He thought — fucking Intel.

Pim exited the vehicle and shook the hand of a senior soldier before turning to another to repeat the same process.

Trigger pressure maintained... wind negligible... Target acquired and maintained!

'Once more into the fray' said Devereaux, sotto voce.

Pim turned to the senior officer, and at that moment, Devereaux released the shot, the recoil captured into his shoulder. Then his crosshairs were back on target with the round striking Pim in the centre of the chest, and he buckled backwards, hitting the ground.

ASIS OPS ROOM
CANBERRA

The OPS Room was silent; all eyes were glued to the large monitor on the wall. Stevens and Webb stood looking on as the fatal shot was taken.

'Woah, that was graphic' said Myra.

'I see only one down' Stevens said.

'Myra, can we zoom in on that any further?' Webb asked?

'Sir that's as much as we can go, we are at full magnification.'

Stevens looked at Magnus and then back at the screen.

'Looks like we only have one target down. What the hell happened?'

'Well, the int said that Pim and Getti would be there, but we already know the information has not been accurate – like the two dozen soldiers that weren't meant to be there. Given the man down is the only one being attended to, and there is not a team trying to usher the other target away - my guess is that he took the shot at the only target there was' Webb suggested.

'You mean that only one target was present on-site? Or that he didn't have a shot on the second target?' Stevens turned and asked.

'Looking at the situation as it happened on screen, one would think there would be a hell of a commotion going one with the other target as in protecting him from the sniper.'

'Yes, you are probably right, but that leaves us with a dilemma, doesn't it?' said Stevens.

'That most certainly does' Webb responded. 'And by the look of it, the Asset has his hands full judging by the way those soldiers are deploying – The hunter is now the prey.' Webb added as he looked at Stevens.

CAMBODIA

Devereaux noted that Pim continued to move on the ground. At the same time, his troops spread out to take cover, looking in all directions

for the shooter. Devereaux released another shot, this time striking Pim in the head, just above the right ear. Pim's head exploded as the round tore through his skull, a pink mist of blood filtering through the immediate area.

Gunfire erupted, with shots flying in all directions, but it was clear they didn't have a fix on Devereaux's location.

Reaching down, he pressed the send button on his SATCOM and waited until the transmission had been sent.

Shoving the SATCOM into his backpack and collecting the two spent cartridge cases, Devereaux began his sterilisation and withdrawal sequence. He headed in a westward direction through the jungle and onward towards the Thai border some 12 kilometres away.

Sporadic gunfire continued as Devereaux moved along his escape route, the first kilometre must be swift to gain distance between him and anyone who pursued. But it must also be made with great care, as Devereaux had not yet trod this ground.

The primary jungle was perfect for quick movement, with sparse secondary growth that would typically make progress slow and noisy. However, this type of forest, with a canopy 60m above was so thick, that it limited the amount of sunlight through, and thus starved the secondary growth of the light it needed to thrive.

While Devereaux no longer had visual on the killing area, he could hear what sounded like trucks entering the area and other, lighter vehicles moving to the south and north.

Devereaux would need to pick up his pace to put some distance between himself and the KR, which was now searching for him.

Five minutes ago, Pim was Devereaux's prey, but the page had turned, and now Devereaux was the hunted.

As he moved through the jungle, Devereaux pondered why Getti was not on site.

His mission was a partial success as far as Devereaux was concerned, but he knew he could not help bad Intel.

With a little finesse, however, this could have a beneficial spin, he thought, with Pim lured to a rendezvous with Getti where Getti failed to turn up, and then Pim got whacked! Maybe there is a positive outcome to this story as it may sow the seed of mistrust amongst the KR and Getti's faction and take away suspicion from outside intervention.

Making the ridgeline, which ran east-west, he followed the ridge towards the Thai border, now 11 kilometres away. This move, he estimated, would take him two days of moving semi-tactically, but would depend on the ferocity of his pursuers. He knew he needed to pick up the pace to put plenty of distance between him and the killing area.

Devereaux could see the jungle foliage parting about 50m ahead, wisps of light plunging from the sky through the canopy above to create a curtain of light.

He knelt and observed the area, looking in all direction for a safe place to cross the small dirt track, which was capable of vehicle movement. He noted this track was not visible on the aerial photographs he had studied before the mission. Suddenly, he could hear a vehicle labouring up the hill to the south. As he scanned the area, a faded red truck slowly breached the crest of the hill; on the rear tray, there were at least 12 men armed with AK-47's and RPG's.

A command rang out, and two men jumped off the back of the truck and began to walk along the track as the vehicle continued, dropping another two men 200m further down the track. They were attempting to cordon the region to capture or kill the shooter. Devereaux remained perfectly still as the two passed him by, looking on either side of the road. Devereaux slowly removed his backpack – no sudden movements. Releasing two nylon straps, he removed his Heckler & Koch MP5-SD and resecured the straps on his pack. His MP5-SD was a suppressed weapon, so it would not give away his position if he were to engage. He made the MP5-SD ready and continued to survey the area.

Looks clear, he thought. Devereaux removed the Carl Zeiss scope from his PSG-1 and slid it into the top of his pack.

They'll be back soon, so it's time to dump some unneeded gear, he thought.

Removing the bolt from the rifle and placing it in his trouser pocket, he cachéd the PSG-1 in a hollowed-out log on the ground, ensuring the weapon was camouflaged so that he could move faster.

Devereaux now only had his MP5-SD and a Silenced High Standard pistol as well as a survival knife, which he wore on a belt strap in the middle of his lower back.

He would have to abandon all of his equipment before he crossed the border to avoid being arrested and suspected of having any association with Pim's death.

Devereaux heard a noise off to the right and immediately froze.

Devereaux spotted two men walking 20m off and parallel to the track. They were sweeping the edge of the track for any signs of the shooter. KR - mid-thirties, Devereaux suspected, with their weapons on their shoulders and not at the ready. Their course was directly towards him!

Devereaux slowly raised his MP5-SD, and as they reached 10m, Devereaux fired two rounds in quick succession, striking the first KR in the left cheek and left the eye.

Before the second soldier could remove his weapon from his shoulder, Devereaux fired another two rounds, both entering his forehead just above his right brow.

They toppled backward and lifeless before hitting the ground. Devereaux couldn't remain there any longer – their disappearance would quickly be noted. He hastily camouflaged the bodies and moved close to the track, crossing it quickly.

Just as he crossed it, the world around him exploded as a burst from an AK-47 ripped up the jungle behind him. Devereaux sprinted into the jungle, changing direction as he made his way deeper into the rainforest, rounds cracking behind him as the bullets passed him by.

Trees and bark exploded into fragments and showered him with debris as he pushed deeper into the jungle and away from the track.

Shouting erupted, and he could hear his pursuers running after him. Devereaux stopped to listen and heard at least three people. The indiscriminate fire continued and whistle-blasts, signalling that the trackers had found their prey and calling others to the hunt, pierced the rainforest.

Devereaux broke cover, engaging a KR 5m away. His rounds hit the KR in the centre of his chest. Staying low, he weaved his way through the foliage before crouching behind a large tree.

A loud bang and a whooshing sound passed overhead quickly followed by a loud explosion 30m behind him. The blast knocked him to the ground. While scrambling to his feet and continuing to sprint away, Devereaux engaged a soldier carrying an RPG. The soldier was hit in the thigh, but not incapacitated.

Devereaux changed again, putting distance between himself and his last location. The soldier reloaded his RPG and engaged again, sending the grenade directly into the tree that Devereaux had just used for cover.

Devereaux again changed direction, zigzagging his way through the jungle. Whistle blasts permeated the area with commands directing the maneuver screamed through the air.

Slowing his pace so that he could hear his hunters, Devereaux knew that he would have to break contact as soon as possible and slow to a tactical speed to allow him the opportunity to slip away silently.

As Devereaux moved around a larger tree, he came face to face with a KR soldier, literally within arm's length. Devereaux grabbed the soldier, preventing him from raising his weapon. They struggled against each other in fierce hand-to-hand combat.

Both men fell to the ground, and the young KR managed to get on top of Devereaux, trying to strangle him. Devereaux searched for the handle of his knife,

41

grasping it and quickly thrusting the blade into the upper arm of his opponent, neatly severing the brachial artery and tendons.

The Soldier screamed in agony as Devereaux pushed him to the side and thrust the same blade into the soldier's neck, bringing his enemy to silence.

The third strike was sent directly into the soldier's heart, extinguishing any further sign of life.

Devereaux had no time to stop. He crawled away and paused for a few seconds, listening for any sign of the enemy nearby and trying to calm himself before moving off again.

Devereaux could hear distant sounds only, estimating that the enemy was at least 100m away. He moved west to break contact while continuously changing direction and pausing regularly to listen. Whistle-blasts were getting further away — he had thrown them off track this time. Devereaux continued his move towards the Thai border for the next 4 hours without further contact.

Distant sounds could be heard, but nothing to cause immediate concern.

As the night would soon be upon him, he stopped and established his night Laying Up Point (LUP). His LUP would have to provide him with an early warning from anyone approaching and would have to offer at least two escape routes given the day's events. Selecting his LUP, Devereaux moved into position and sat leaning up against a tree, his MP5-SD across his legs. As last light fell, Devereaux sat listening for any movement emanating from his surroundings – any sign that would indicate he was still being followed.

The task, however, was made impossible by the jungle noises that only increased as day turned to night. The night provided Devereaux with a reprise from the last 48hrs, and he needed some rest before going for the border early the next day.

By his estimate, he was only 6kms from the border, as today's activity saw him cover a sizable distance.

The tactical environment would only allow him to eat high-energy food bars and some dehydrated fruit. He drank a litre of water to maintain hydration and spent the next few hours listening, trying to pick up any sign of movement. As he rested, he took time to reload all of his magazines and to give his weapon a tactical clean. He refilled his water bottles from the bladder in his pack. He added an electrolyte mix to the remaining water in the bladder and drank it.

As he sat up against the tree, the MP5-SD across his thighs, Devereaux thought back over the day and what ultimately lead him to his current position.

His termination of Pim didn't cause him any distress at all. He remembered that, when he squeezed the trigger, his heart rate was calm — a steady pulse that was unbroken by the moment.

His breathing at that very point in time was steady and rhythmic. He wondered what kind of person he was? It was a clinical question really, more than an emotional one.

Was he cold-hearted? No, he thought to himself, far from it. He was SAS, a professional to the core - his objective would always be achieved.

Did that make him a machine, he wondered?

A loud crashing sound echoed through the jungle, and the area fell silent. Deadfall, he thought to himself. He closed his eyes and dozed off into a shallow sleep, subconsciously filtering noises that were not part of the jungle's soundtrack.

The night passed quickly, and he soon awoke at 0430hrs, with the sun still left with sixty minutes to raise its head. He sat there, listening for any sound or sign of movement.

Devereaux then knelt and urinated off to one side before sitting back against the tree, waiting quietly as the sun began to rise.

As the sun rose, it cast an auburn light through the primary canopy, and the background hum of the jungle steadily increased in volume.

Glancing down at his watch, Devereaux noted it was 0550hrs and time to move towards the border.

Slowly hoisting his pack onto his back, he tightened the straps and carefully scanned the area before maneuvering himself to his knees.

He scanned the area once again before finally standing.

He looked around at where he was sleeping to ensure that he had not left anything behind. He then carefully camouflaged the site and moved to the west, following the ridgeline. He moved very slowly, placing each step with care to ensure he made no sound or left any sign that he was there. He continued to scan the area, periodically stopping and looking back along the way he came to ensure no one was following him up. At each brief stop, he would listen for about 60 seconds, trying to hear any noise that would indicate he wasn't alone.

Devereaux froze, instinctively, when he heard a noise off to the right. As he peered through the foliage, he saw three KR moving parallel to him and about 40m away. They looked like they were walking along a footpad type track, which Devereaux had not seen the evening before.

A burst of fire came from the right! A fourth KR straggler had seen Devereaux and opened fire from about 50m, with two rounds striking the side of Devereaux's pack.

Devereaux didn't return fire – he didn't want to show the other three KR where he was – but rather crouched over and ran, trying to break the contact as silently as possible.

The movement, slight as it was, caught the eye of a second KR and the fight was on. Devereaux reached into his pouch and took out a grenade pulled the pin and threw it in the direction of the closest KR to slow down their closure.

The sound of the exploding grenade was immense, and a scream echoed through the jungle as the wounded KR cried in agony. Devereaux saw another soldier approaching from the left and engaged him with a well-aimed burst of fire to the chest. At this point, whistle blasts rang through the air both near and far – the call to action was on.

Devereaux started to move south, changing direction as often as possible. His backpack was slowing him down, an issue Devereaux would have to deal with sooner rather than later. He paused to listen and could hear someone, not too far away, coming in his direction. He decided to wait and ambush whoever was following him. Intermittent flashes of light caught Devereaux's attention, and his hunter was almost there. With his MP5-SD at the ready, he waited until the KR was virtually on top of him before he engaged. Devereaux fired two rounds in quick succession, striking the KR in the chest and causing him to collapse at Devereaux's feet. As Devereaux looked down, he noticed that the KR was only a child, not more than 15 or 16 years old. As he looked into the boy's eyes, he could see his pupils dilating as his life bled out of him, blood frothing from his mouth and nose as the last air in his lungs was exhaled. Hearing more noise off to the right, Devereaux quickly removed the boy's chest webbing and collected the AK-47 and continued to move south.

Before he changed direction again, he decided to dump his pack so that he could move faster and more freely.

Instead, he would use only a small day pack secured to the top of his pack by four black plastic clips - but he wouldn't leave his pack as a trophy for his pursuers.

Devereaux found an LUP and began preparing his pack for destruction, occasionally glancing up to survey the area.

He carried a White Phosphorous (WP) grenade, some blasting fuse connected to a detonator and fitted with an M60 Igniter to set the fuse in motion. He removed essential items from the pack, including additional ammunition and the small waterproof daypack containing a change of clothing and the documents he would need when he crossed the border. Everything else went into the pack and, after preparing the WP grenade; he placed it flush against the SATCOM, laying the fuse so that the M60 Igniter was easily assessable from the outside of the pack. He had escaped again, but for how long? Devereaux had been on the move for an hour since killing the boy, and he badly needed hydration, rest, and to get his thoughts together.

Finding a thickly wooded outcrop of bamboo, which was dim and provided excellent cover from observation, Devereaux set himself up, so he was comfortable and took time to rest.

In the distance, he could hear the movement of vehicles and, now and then, automatic fire.

It sounded like AK-47's being fired at least 500m away. It was nice knowing they were that far away, but unsettling that they had not given up the chase.

Suddenly, Devereaux heard noises. It was a motorcycle – no, wait... two motorcycles. He rolled his eyes in disbelief and got himself ready to move. Looking through the foliage, he could see four men, two on each bike, and all armed with AK's.

The riders stopped 40m away and began to chat as Devereaux quickly reassessed his escape route.

The soldiers got off of the motorcycles and continued chatting, oblivious to Devereaux's presence. This was an opportunity to create a diversion, drawing other KR to the south, and giving Devereaux a chance to head northwest and across the border. Devereaux positioned his pack in the centre of the LUP, and then pulled the M60 Igniter attached to the WP Grenade.

He immediately emptied a 30-round magazine from the AK-47 he had taken from the boy directly into the group of four, hitting at least two in the process before turning and running like hell through the rainforest, dumping the now empty AK in the process.

A large volume of fire erupted, and the LUP was torn to shreds. Devereaux was long gone, and the fuse was still burning down.

Two KR carefully walked towards the LUP, noting that they did not receive any return fire. Maybe they had killed the shooter?

A third KR, who was wounded in the initial burst from Devereaux, began to follow his colleagues, limping as he closed cautiously on the LUP.

Entering the bamboo cluster, they spread out about 2m apart searching for Devereaux. All of a sudden, there was a massive explosion and plume of white phosphorous spreading everywhere in the cluster. The white phosphorous, sticking to all three KR and burning them intensely. Screams bellowed through the jungle as it went to work. Within seconds the cries of agony went silent.

Devereaux's pack and equipment were totally destroyed, and the four KR had been neutralised.

Devereaux moved in a westerly direction after the explosion, and after 300m, he turned back northward, hoping to bypass any follow-up action by the KR.

Devereaux paused to listen and to scour the direction ahead. As he was observing, he reached down with one hand and released the clip on his ammunition pouch.

He removed the magazine on his MP5-SD and placed it next to him and then, withdrew a full magazine from the pouch and placed it in the weapon.

Picking up the magazine from the ground, he reloaded it and placed it back inside the pouch. He was careful not to make a sound, or even to take his eyes off of the terrain around him. Closing the clip on his ammunition pouch, he carefully stood up and continued to make his way through the jungle.

Two hours later, Devereaux crossed a small creek and replenished his water bladder and poured the cool water over his head before continuing up a hill and positioning himself on a ridge overlooking a valley that ran north-south.

At the bottom of the valley was a small tributary connecting further south into a larger river. From here, it was 2.2kms to the Thai border, but it was the most dangerous part of his exfiltration, as the KR had not given up their pursuit. If he were to hurry here, he would no doubt be compromised. Devereaux decided to take a ten-minute rest and evaluate his position and circumstances.

Looking through the Carl Zeiss scope, he could see the route he needed to take as well as all approach points to the selected route across the border. There on the valley below, moving from north to south was a group of six KR patrolling along the river's edge.

Their pace was fast; it seemed that Devereaux's diversion was working, by drawing troops south.

A motorcycle, with what looked like a man in his 20s, stopped to talk with the KR. Soon after, they moved on, heading further south along the valley, Devereaux stood slowly and moved down a ridgeline closer to the river where he had seen a possible crossing point. He maintained surveillance on the crossing point, noting two further patrols had passed over the last four hours, all heading south. Devereaux decided he would attempt to cross the river and open ground once night fell. The night seemed to take forever to arrive. Devereaux took a deep breath and told himself to slow down and reset his mind so that his eagerness wouldn't get himself killed.

As night fell, he approached the river's edge and took one last look before entering the water. He pushed a small floatation device made from his water bladder and some bamboo to assist in floatation. On top of the floatation device and resting in front of him, his MP5-SD was at the ready. As he got to the other side, he heard two people talking just to the right of his position.

The two villagers chatted as they walked along a dirt road parallel to the river, unaware of Devereaux's presence.

After they passed, Devereaux emerged from the river and carefully moved across the dirt track and into the jungle on the other side as silently as he could. Moving purely on compass bearing and distance, he found a suitable LUP and prepared for the night. His position was elevated so that he could keep a view on the valley below. Dim lights emanating along the track and up the valley, no doubt coming from candles and torchlights of local people going about their business.

The darkness engulfed Devereaux, and he knew he was not safe yet, but rather at a critical time of his mission. Tomorrow's river crossing would be vital - the river was all that divided Cambodia and Thailand.

He couldn't afford any mistakes, and as a result, left him with so many thoughts and contingencies to consider. As he sat leaning up against the trunk of a tree, he thought about the boy; he had no option but to kill.

He could see the boy in his mind's eye so clearly as he remembered those dark brown eyes and how the life disappeared from them.

A kid, he thought, what the fuck! For the first time on this mission, Devereaux felt human. Those eyes were vivid, and the scene played over in his mind. Could I have tried something different? He thought to himself.

Would he have been able to merely subdue him, to ultimately spare him? No, down that path lay madness.

Devereaux's shoulders dropped, and he exhaled slowly. Of course, there was no other way, and he resigned himself to that fact, but the knot in his stomach was a reminder of that deed of survival.

The night had passed by so quickly. 0350hrs already, Devereaux thought to himself.

Leaning against a tree, Devereaux listened to the jungle as familiar sounds echoed through the rainforest – and yet there were also unfamiliar sounds. A primate he had never heard before, was calling out that dawn was almost here and was signalling that this was his territory.

At 0430hrs, Devereaux was already on the move, executing all his patrol skills to ensure he had not left any sign. Each step must be deliberate, each movement in slow motion to reduce noise. 500m to the Thai border, then on to Bangkok and home, he thought to himself. Devereaux reached the river's edge, scanned the area one last time before lowering himself into the water up to his neck, and listening for any sign of activity.

He began swimming across the river, which was about 100m across. At 30m from the Thai side of the river, all hell broke loose. Bursts of small firearms tore up the river behind him and the bank ahead.

'Fuck!' Devereaux exclaimed as he ducked under the water. Torchlight was frantically scouring the water, looking everywhere for its prey, voices screaming commands.

Devereaux emerged silently 20m further down the river and closer to the bank before submerging once again to avoid detection.

While under the water he released his grip on his MP5-SD and let it sink to the bottom of the river. As he emerged, he drew out his High Standard silent pistol and slid up the bank and into the jungle. Intermittent gunfire was still occurring as the KR desperately continued their search.

Devereaux moved away from the river's edge as quickly as possible - eager to put as much space between him and the border and any Thai patrols that happened by.

Finding a place to rest up, he changed into a pair of denim jeans, a black t-shirt and some sneakers. He slid a plastic bag containing a Passport, US$1,000 and 2000 Thai Baht down his shirt and buried the pistol and remaining clothes and equipment.

After camouflaging the area, he moved off northward and disappeared into the Thai landscape.

CHAPTER 4

'Contact'

1991: QUEENSCLIFF, VICTORIA.

A plume of mist pierced the cold night air as the warm breath escaped from Devereaux's mouth. He walked slowly along the poorly paved footpath as he tried to avoid the water-filled potholes. As he entered a telephone booth, he noticed the dim glow of streetlights being gently filtered by the clinging mist and persistent fine drizzle. Closing the door behind him, he searched for some loose change in his pocket; lifted the handset and dropped two coins into the slot and dialled a number. Before the number was answered, he pressed down on the receiver terminating the call. He remained inside the phone booth as if he was having a telephone conversation, and remained there for the approximate time it would take to actually order a taxi.

He replaced the receiver, collected his coins and then stepped back out into the cold night air. of the wooden bench.

Devereaux could see the vehicle had stopped and was parked on the side of the road - about 150m from the bus stop. He could see the driver had switched on the interior light and was searching for something.

Turning up the collar on his old heavy winter coat, he sat down on the frost-covered bench and waited for his taxi.

Headlights from an approaching vehicle disturbed the darkness of the bus shelter, and a small red Ford Laser came to a halt in front of him. He slid his hand into his coat pocket and activated a micro-recorder that was sewn into the lining of his coat.

Devereaux looked up and saw the passenger window open, the interior light revealing the inside of the car. A young woman released her seat belt and leaned across the passenger seat and beckoned towards him.

'Excuse me, sir' said a soft voice.

'I seem to be somewhat lost. I'm trying to find the shortest way to the Geelong cinema,' she added.

Devereaux leaned forward on his seat and said, 'That's not surprising, these streets can be confusing at times.'

'I'm actually going to meet some friends at the Geelong Hotel, which is only 50 metres from the cinema, but I'm waiting for my taxi to arrive,' Devereaux said.

The girl looked up at him and said, 'In that case, I can save you the cab fare if you would be kind enough to show me the way.'

Devereaux looked at the girl intently, then stood up and moved towards the vehicle, casually panning up and down the street before stepping into the car and closing the door behind him. 'Right' said Devereaux in a menacing voice, 'turn that fucking interior light off and slowly pull away from the curb, then take a left at the second intersection. Bloody amateurs!' he barked. The girl looked at him, then reached up and closed the light. The interior fell into darkness with only the instruments issuing a pale green glow and the occasional intermittent flicker of a streetlight as they passed by.

'Who the fuck are you, and where is Dylan?' he asked with an annoyed tone. The girl looked at him, visibly startled by his abrupt question.

'Dylan had to return to Canberra on some urgent business and asked me to do this meet,' she said.

'He said you were aware of such contingencies and that this may happen from time to time – that you would understand the importance of maintaining such a rendezvous.'

'I see' Devereaux replied.

He glanced at the girl and asked, 'did he have a message for me?'

The girl turned towards him and saw him glancing intentionally at her well-formed breasts. He looked up at her and stared directly into her eyes without any embarrassment of being caught.

She returned his stare and then issued a teasing smirk and then turned her attention back to the road and said.

'Yes, in fact, he asked me to tell you that Blue Star Airline shares are a good buy.'

'He said you would understand what he means,' she added.

Dylan and Devereaux had developed a series of authentication codes for just such occasions.

'My name's Rachel,' she said in a soft but confident manner.

'Were you shadowed?' she said.

'No, it looks clean, but –'

Rachel cuts him off in mid-sentence.

'Before you go on any further, if we get pulled over, our cover story will be in line with our authentication phrase and the counter phrase, OK?'

'You needed to get to the Geelong Hotel, and I wanted to go to the cinema', she added.

'OK, sounds reasonable', he said with a smile and noted that she didn't ask him to continue what he was saying before she interrupted him.

Devereaux peered over towards her and noticed how young she looked, remembering they were never this young when he started in this game. John Devereaux, a 43-year-old career SAS man who was married with two children. His hair, once a dark brown colour, was slowly greying, something he put down to the stresses of SAS life.

Devereaux's jaw was square. His eyes a crystal blue and his complexion fair, something he felt cursed with living under the harsh Australian sun, especially being of Viking stock.

He was 180 centimetres tall, and although he kept in good shape, his body was starting to feel the worse for wear. The years of lugging a huge rucksack and torturing his body to near breaking point were beginning to show.

She wore a soft, white sheer blouse with two buttons purposely undone to reveal a black lacy bra designed to persuade any man she came in contact with. Her long, honey-blonde hair cascaded over her shoulders and her perfectly sculptured facial features hinted of Scandinavian ancestry.

At 22, she was undoubtedly what the Service wanted: a highly intelligent, articulate, beautiful and very confident woman. Rachel knew what she had and how to manipulate it to get what she wanted – something she had no doubt done all her life.

Devereaux glanced over and saw the light shining on her red lips and her matching nail polish on her long fingernails. She wore a short skirt, which rode up high as she sat down behind the steering wheel. He was not impressed with her presentation, as he knew that if she turned up dressed like that in Moscow or in a Middle Eastern, she might encounter difficulties with certain contacts, that may very well love to have their way with her. Devereaux had known a former Intelligence Officer operating in Kyiv, who had made the same mistake and paid for it with her honour after her Russian Mafia contact that she was meeting on a counter-weapons proliferation mission, decided that he would rape her instead.

Devereaux knew, of course, that there were times when this type of presentation was necessary and highly useful, but not when you are making contact with an agent for the first time, and especially not when operating on your own in secluded locations.

As the vehicle continued through the countryside, passing farms and densely wooded outcrops, Devereaux checked the side mirror.

'I'm not sure, but I think we have a tail,' he said.

Rachel glanced up at her mirror and said, 'Yes, two vehicles are working as a team'.

'Shit!' said Devereaux.

'If I get caught, I'll be off to prison, or maybe even killed for this shit!' he added with some intensity.

'What the fuck are you going to do about this?' he yelled, hoping to apply some pressure on her. Rachel glanced across at him. 'Relax, I'll try and lose them at the next turn and take an alternate route.'

Rachel planted her foot on the accelerator, and the vehicle pulled away.

'The fuck you will!' snapped Devereaux.

'We have a perfectly good cover story in place.'

'You'll just create additional suspicion and attract their attention, so stick to our plan' he added.

'OK, OK', Rachel retorted as she rechecked the mirror.

'Reduce your speed and maintain the speed limit,' Devereaux said.

Rachel eased off of the accelerator and brought the needle back to 70 km per hour.

Rachel looked over at Devereaux with more intent and said, 'Alright, enough fun and games – let's get to business, what have you got for me?'

Devereaux took another glance in the mirror and saw the lead surveillance vehicle peel off. The second vehicle takes over the tail.

'I have two rolls of 400 ISO film shot at F8 for you' he said. 'Both rolls of film contain photographs of documents of the Pakistan Government's agreement and intentions to supply uranium to North Korea in November of this year'.

'Jesus, Devereaux' Rachel replied.

'What date were the documents signed and by whom?'

'They were signed by the Minister of External Affairs and are dated three days ago' he said.

'Devereaux' Rachel said, 'That's great work. Dylan said that you always came up with the goods. In fact, he said your product was first-rate, and your work is always very professional.' Devereaux glanced over at her and forced a smile, as he was often amused when an Intelligence Officer was trying to blow sunshine up his arse!

'Thanks, Rachel, that's always good to hear.'

'In the compartment between our seats is an empty drink bottle. Wrap the film in that tissue paper and place the film in the bottle. Stuff a few extra pieces of loose tissue paper in on top of it and secure the lid' Rachel said.

Devereaux opened the compartment and started to do as she had asked when he asked, 'Have you got my money?'

Rachel checked the review mirror once again and noted the tail had turned off to the right.

'Yes,' she replied.

'Open the glove compartment, and you will see a Time magazine. On pages 30 through to 40 you will find $100 notes slipped in between each page' she replied. Devereaux picked up the magazine and rolled it up and placed it into his pocket.

'I told Dylan that the price for such information had gone up. Where are the additional funds?' he said.

Rachel looked over at him wide-eyed and visibly uneasy and said, 'Dylan didn't mention it to me. I'm sure that he has plans to discuss such an increase with Canberra. In fact, I'm sure that's one of his priorities and will be discussing with the Assistant Director', she added confidently.

Devereaux turned to her and said, 'OK, well, if I don't get $5,000 in green for each and every drop in the future, I'm out of here, and you can find your precious shit somewhere else'.

'Do you think I'm stupid or something?' he added.

'I'm the one taking all the risks while you sit on your arse under the safety of your diplomatic umbrella. So, if you want anything more from me, it's $5,000 each time we meet, and I want the balance for this pickup, OK?'

Rachel looked over at him, a little less confident than she had been before, as she knew she couldn't make that kind of decision at her level.

'OK, I'll send off a message to Dylan and ask him to address your requirements' she said.

'Take the next turn to the left. This is the Bellarine Highway, and it will take us into town' he said. Rachel slowed the vehicle and proceeded to merge left and then began to accelerate. She noticed a car that was parked on the side of the road turn on its headlights. It pulled out on to the road and began to follow them, maintaining a distance of about 100 metres.

'We have that tail again' Rachel said.

'OK, just keep an eye on it and stick to the speed limit and obey all the road rules' he said.

'Devereaux' Rachel said, as she glanced up again into the rear vision mirror.

'I need you to follow up on the information you have given me tonight. In particular, dates of shipment, quantities, costs, and authorising bodies from within Pakistan and North Korean Governments.'

Devereaux looked over at her and said, 'OK, I don't think that will be too difficult a task – but I'm not doing a thing until I get confirmation that my fees will be met.'

'I want an answer by Friday of this week, and I want it delivered to Dead Letter Box (DLB) Alpha', he added.

'There is no room for negotiation here, Rachel – just do it, or I won't be at the next pick up' he said with defiance. Rachel breathed heavily with obvious annoyance at his demands.

'OK, I'll contact you at the DLB on Friday.'

'In the meantime, chase up the information we need, Devereaux,' she said in a more irritated tone.

'I'm sure that Dylan will look after your needs' she added. 'Can we meet again? Maybe on Monday of next week?'

'OK, where do you want to meet?' he replied.

'I think we should use the cinema. I'll go into the cinema one and sit in the second row from the rear, on the far left-hand side.' She said.

'We should go to the 10:00am session, as the movie has been playing for some time now, so there shouldn't be too many people there.'

Devereaux glanced over at her and asked, 'what movie are you talking about?'

'Oh sorry, it's called Jurassic Park'.

'As we know each other by sight, there will be no need for the usual authentication phrases, but we should have a safety signal just in case,' she said.

'How about I wear a baseball cap and if I still continue to wear it when you approach me, that means it's safe, and you should continue the contact? And if it's unsafe, I will remove the cap', Rachel responded.

'OK, that sounds good, and if I think it is not safe, I'll proceed to the front row and sit down Devereaux added.

'Alright' said Rachel. 'Leave a seat empty between us and I'll leave my bag on it so you can drop the product into it, OK?'

'Make sure my payment is there in full, or you'll have me to contend with' he said in a less-than-friendly tone.

Rachel looked at him and knew he was not kidding.

'OK, Devereaux' she said.

'Alright, we are about two minutes out from the cinema. Is the tail still there?'

Rachel glanced up and couldn't see the vehicle any longer.

'No, I think they have dropped us' she remarked.

'So how is your family doing, Devereaux? Is there anything you need for them?'

Devereaux looked over and was surprised that she would ask such a loaded question when he had just demanded such a substantial rise in his fee.

He knew she was just going through the drill, but was fascinated with her question nonetheless and thought he could have some fun with this young one but refrained as the drop point was not far away. She needed to get the procedure down pat, rather than grappling with lessons already covered during their transit.

68

'My family is fine, Rachel, and we don't really need anything at this stage' he said.

'But thank you for asking,' he added.

'Take the next turn to the right, then the second to the left into Moorable Street, the cinema is about a kilometre up on the right'.

'Yeah, I know where I am. I'll approach at about 50km per hour and slow just outside the hotel and stop about 20 metres past the main entrance, OK?' Rachel said as she began her drop off drill.

'That sounds fine to me' he said.

'When I pull over at the curb, get out of the car and close the door immediately. Walk to the rear of the vehicle and across the road, then go straight into the hotel and wait there for at least 30 minutes before leaving' she said.

'I will drive up to the front of the cinema and park my car somewhere close by, and go inside', she added. 'Whatever you do, stand clear of the car as I pull away. I don't want any accident happening to you. So, are you clear as to what we are about to do?' she said.

Devereaux looked in the mirror and then looked back at her and said, 'Of course, I've done this many times with Dylan, and I know the drill' he said with a smug tone.

'OK, 10 seconds.'

'Thanks, Devereaux' Rachel added.

The vehicle slowed to a halt as she had said and Devereaux opened the car door and stepped out on to the pavement. He closed the door and turned and walked to the rear of the car and crossed the street. Devereaux could see Rachel's car as it turned the corner and disappeared from sight.

Devereaux entered the hotel and made his way to the bar and ordered a Corona and then moved to the rear of the bar and pulled up a seat. He reached inside his pocket and turned off the micro- recorder and eased himself back into the comfortable leather chair. Glancing up at the old clock on the wall just above the bar, he could see that it was 9:58pm.

He panned around the mostly deserted bar and noticed a man entering from a side entrance which led out to an alleyway. He wore a pair of military-style trousers with the pockets on the side. His heavy overcoat was old and tattered and had seen better days. Still, it was perfect for the weather that was presently gripping the Geelong region.

He watched the man move to the bar and, as the light from the bar caught his face, Devereaux could see that it was Lochlan Connor. Connor had been with ASIS for some 30 years and had clocked much of his experience operating in the shadows in Europe and Far East Asia. His thin, wiry frame and seemingly timid demeanour covered a highly intelligent and super fit man for his age.

Connor was a biochemist and a marathon runner, and who had a very sharp mind. He was gifted with a photographic memory, which pissed Devereaux off as Devereaux often joked he had trouble remembering what he did yesterday.

Connor was a man of many overseas assignments in the former USSR, Czech Republic, Israel, Spain, Myanmar, and Thailand.

Connor collected his scotch and walked across the room and pulled up a chair next to Devereaux and said. 'Hello, old son... did you have fun?'

Devereaux looked up with a smirk and said, 'just like old times, Connor!'

'Have you got the tape for me?' asked Connor. Devereaux reached into his pocket and removed the tape from the micro-recorder and handed it across to Connor.

'Thanks' Connor replied.

Devereaux looked up and said, 'nothing else I would rather be doing on a night as shitty as this. The weather hasn't eased up for the past few days.'

'I hear you Dev, roll on summer,' Connor said then took a sip of his whiskey.

'So how did she go?' Connor asked.

'I think she did quite well, of course, there is some honing to do on the basics, and importantly, I think you need to talk to her about the way she dresses for the occasion. She needs to be given a few home truths about the dangers of dressing to impress, especially with her outstanding cleavage' Devereaux grinned.

'And that it is' Connor replied.

'Seriously, she needs to be made aware of the appropriate times for such things – and tonight, with a new agent she had never met, it could have ended badly for her. Remember Andrea in Kyiv?' he added.

Connor looked across at him and said, 'You're right, of course. I'll chat with her in the morning.'

'You'll be able to get a better picture from the tape, but another area of concern was her readiness to move away from her cover story. What I mean is, when she realised that there was a surveillance team on her tail, she was all for making it into a car chase. However, I put her straight there, but you may want to reinforce that issue', Devereaux said.

'What was her manner like?' asked Connor.

'I thought she was quite good, actually. She was rather pleasant and noncommittal to my demands for more funds', Devereaux said with a smile. 'I would also talk to her about not setting a pattern.' 'When we discussed the location for the next meeting, she wanted to use the cinema again. She needs to get such patterns out of her head, or she will set herself up to be compromised', he added.

'By the end of the course, you should have a good IO on your hands.'

'OK, thanks, mate. I appreciate your time and assistance tonight. It's good to have you in these activities – you bring great experience to the table. You've proven to be a most valuable asset' Connor said.

Surely this can't be the end of the debrief, Devereaux thought. Such debriefs usually went on for at least an hour or two. What's going on here? He pondered.

Devereaux looked over at the window and then turned back again at Connor, raising his glass and asking in a cautious tone, 'Thanks Connor, but that's not really the reason you asked me to participate in this exercise, is it?'

Connor shifted his gaze over at Devereaux and looked intently at him for a few seconds before picking up his scotch and taking a rather large swig.

73

'Cheers... You're a smart prick aren't you Dev?' Connor said with a cheeky grin. Devereaux raised his glass.

'Yes, I am. I'm sorry, Connor, it's an irreparable flaw in my character' he said with a somewhat winning smile. Devereaux continued his stare in silence, waiting for Connor to continue.

'Bilateral discussions were held last Wednesday between the Minister for Foreign Affairs and Trade and the Minister for Defence in regards to military involvement in a task we need to have conducted' Connor said.

Devereaux looked across the room at the barmaid who was holding up a glass to see if they wanted any more drinks. Devereaux nodded, and she began to pour another Scotch.

'So what do you want with me?' he asked curiously.

Connor glanced down at his empty glass and then looked back up to meet Devereaux's eyes.

'Since the cock-up at the Sheraton Hotel, you're aware that the Service has not been conducting a great deal of Black Ops and we're somewhat at a loss in this area' he replied.

'The only black bag Op we've conducted since the Sheraton was the Op you ran in Cambodia in 1990. To be quite frank, I put forward your name as the most capable, and to be quite honest, the Service feels comfortable with you', he added.

Devereaux casually raised the fingers on his right-hand signalling Connor to cease the conversation as the young barmaid arrived with their drinks. Connor placed a twenty-dollar note on her tray and said to keep the change. The barmaid smiled and walked away, and both men looked at her well-formed rear, then turned towards each other and smiled.

'Damn that's nice' said Connor.

'So, Dev, old boy', he added, 'you have the most experience working with the Service and know-how we operate.'

'Both Ministers and, indeed, the Chief of the Defence Force (CDF) agree that you're the best man for the job' he added.

'Is that right?' Devereaux replied cautiously.

'John, your SAS background and your experience working with ASIS makes good sense, and you are well suited for the task we have in mind' said Connor.

'Hey, that might be the case, but, what does the Commander Special Operations think about this?' asked Devereaux.

'He has already been advised by the CDF that you have been seconded to his office for the duration and that's all he needs to know.'

'So what's the job, Connor?' Devereaux asked.

'You will be briefed soon enough, John' Connor said.

'I'm heading back to the Island now, do you feel like a few more beers before the night ends?' Connor asked.

'No, I'll head back home and digest the entrée you just served me!' Devereaux said with a tired smile.

'Oh, before we head off, you need to be at the Southern Cross Hotel in Melbourne at 1100hrs tomorrow morning.

We have a briefing with the Service's new Director-General Magnus Webb at 1300hrs, and I want to talk with you further before he arrives' Connor added.

'What's Webb like, Connor?' Devereaux asked.

'Don't worry, you are going to like him – he is pro-Black Ops' Connor replied.

'You can pick up a car from Admin at 0630hrs instead of taking your own vehicle. May as well use the government's fuel, don't you think?' he said as he stood to leave.

Devereaux pulled into the driveway of his Point Lonsdale home and reached forward to turn off the ignition. Sinking back into his seat and resting his head on the headrest, he closed his eyes and thought about what the Firm had in store for him. Opening his eyes, he looked over at the door to the front of the house. In some way, he didn't want to go in as he knew what was to come, something that had been weighing profoundly on his mind. He let out a breath and removed the keys from the ignition, gathered his coat and stepped out into the bitterly cold night air, and walked to the front door. His wife Alisha had the central heating on, and as he felt the warmth of the heater, he was to some extent, pleased to be finally home.

Devereaux hung his coat on the hook in the cloakroom just inside the entrance, then placed his dark grey scarf over the hook and proceeded down the hallway and into a bedroom where his son and daughter were sleeping.

He pulled up the covers on his daughter's bed and kissed her gently on the forehead and then sat on the bed next to his son and watched as they slept.

He wondered what their world would be like in 20 years. Would shadow warriors such as him still be manipulating their future, trying to make it safer, or would the cold war really be over?

Devereaux had been getting tired of the political correctness that was starting to creep into government. He had noticed the softening of political leadership and the lack of moral fibre that seemed to be manifesting itself and becoming more commonplace amongst political parties and within the legal system. Military leaders had been showing similar symptoms, becoming lapdogs for the new breed of politician. Generals are happy to take up the posts and receive massive paychecks as long as they did what they were told. He had concerns about what future his children would have if rough men like himself were not ready to take a stand and fight for our way of life.

Was this the price he had to pay to ensure his children had a future that was free from tyranny, where politicians took a passive mindset to those who would hurt us, and where oligarchs secretly ruled nations? He lay down next to his son and thought about the life they had shared so far. It was full of wonderful times together as they travelled to the countryside, visiting places that were now burned into their memories. As he lay there, his head tilted to one side, he could see the suitcases packed and ready to go, a firm reminder of what was to come in the morning. His children would be going with their mother back to Perth.

Alesha and Devereaux had been married for almost 16 years. Still, they had been growing apart for years now, and the marriage was heavy with unsettled business.

They were still in love with each other of course, or so he thought, but time would surely see them part ways. As Devereaux lay there, he knew that such a life in the shadows was not conducive for a healthy marriage. Such relationships instead, fostered resentment and was like an airport lost and found, where baggage accumulated. In the union with Alesha, such baggage of resentment was always being used in heated discussions, something the pair had become tired of.

When Devereaux had first met Alesha, he had explained that SAS life was particularly tough on married couples with the husband being away for eight to nine months a year on training activities or operations. At the time, Alisha was OK with it, and she was for many years. But bringing up two children alone and not knowing whether her husband was going to return or not, took its toll. For John Devereaux, however, his duty to make the world a better place, a better place for his children, was what drove him to the shadows. The separation, a price he was willing to pay.

He placed his hand on his son's shoulder and drifted off to sleep, still clad in the clothes he had been wearing all that day.

CHAPTER 5

'The Hook'

MELBOURNE.

The Bellarine Highway widened into a dual carriageway as it stretched northward towards Melbourne. The grey sky was typical at this time of year, and the persistent drizzle irritated the hell out of Devereaux. The drive from Queenscliff to Melbourne would take around 2.5 hours in this weather, so Devereaux left at 6:00am to meet with Director-General Magnus Webb at the Southern Cross Hotel on Exhibition Street to discuss matters relating to his assignment.

Devereaux left early so he could observe the Southern Cross Hotel before entering the building. He would look for good escape routes and for individuals who didn't fit the scene. He had learned long ago not to walk into a place that he didn't know how to get out of. This was something he had always done since entering the SAS – it was akin to breathing, something that had become a natural instinct.

Although he was married and had a family, Devereaux had become a solitary man, a practitioner of the cold war, a fact that made him trust no one - not even his own. He wasn't paranoid, but he had learned that in this game, there were no friends, not close friends anyway. He had associates, who often had their own, hidden agendas.

The rain started to ease, and the road became clearer, offering better visibility to about 300 metres.

Devereaux checked his rear-view mirror, then his side mirrors and noticed a blue Ford sedan changing lanes. Nothing too unusual about that, but he also noticed that the vehicle had a small antenna mounted on the roof, the type that was fixed in place by a large magnetic base.

Once again, nothing too unusual about that – except that the blue vehicle changed lanes to allow another Ford sedan, this time a white car, to take its place while the blue car dropped back to about 150 metres. The white vehicle also had a small antenna of the same kind attached to the roof.

A tail, he thought. 'Time to check if I really am paranoid' he said out loud to himself.

He accelerated from 80kmph and watched as the needle climb to 100kmph on the clock, the current speed limit for this stretch of road and maintained that speed for the next 2kms. Looking in his rear vision mirror, he could tell both vehicles had accelerated to preserve their visual contact. Still, the distance between his car and theirs had reduced considerably – surveillance, he thought.

Devereaux noticed a gas station about 300 metres on the left. He decided to test this crew out to see just how good they were. Devereaux's vehicle approached the entrance to the gas station and at about 50 metres out; he trod heavily on his brakes without skidding and turned into the driveway leading into the gas station. Both of the following vehicles braked hard, giving away their intent, before realising their error and then continued past the station, the occupants' attention drawn towards Devereaux's car. He had confirmed his suspicions; they were a surveillance team – amateurs at best, he thought.

After parking the vehicle, he entered the gas station and bought a coffee. Before returning to his car, he peered over some shelving and out through the window of the station. No sign of the surveillance team, so he bought a newspaper and went back to his car.

He looked over the top of his newspaper that was resting on the steering wheel and commenced monitoring the traffic, looking for signs of his tail.

As he sipped on his coffee, he noticed the blue vehicle returning southward on the other side of the highway.

'Interesting' he said to himself.

He swallowed the last of the worst coffee he had ever tasted and reached down, turned the key, bringing life back into the engine.

Devereaux carefully moved the vehicle through the station's parking lot and edged his way out onto the highway before proceeding to accelerate to cruising speed. About 5km further along the road, he saw the white vehicle parked on the side of the road with the hood up.

'Ok, here we go' he thought to himself. He knew he had to lose these guys, but where?

What was their purpose?

Devereaux glanced up to see the Laverton township sign on the side of the road. He had 5km to go before he would arrive – this is where he would have to execute his deception plan.

Taking the off-ramp, he followed the road for another kilometre and found a parking bay outside of a Greek Kebab take-a-way shop. The parking bay was directly outside the main entrance, its windows providing excellent reflective capacity, so he could see behind him. As he sat in his car, casually surveying the area, he glanced up to see the blue vehicle edging its way into the parking lot diagonally across from where he had parked.

Devereaux wore an old double-sided anorak, which was ivory in colour and had a navy-blue interior. The jacket could be turned inside out as it was designed to give two separate options to the wearer.

Devereaux did up the zip on the front of his jacket so that the interior colour couldn't be seen and then exited the car. Locking the door behind him, he made his way into the Kebab shop and stood looking at the drink fridge and then purchased a coke demonstrating some legitimacy for being in the shop.

'Excuse me, do you have a restroom here?'

'Out the back' said the fat Greek tending the Gyros on the vertical rotisserie.

Devereaux made his way to the rear of the shop and went into the restroom, removed his jacket, and turned it inside out and unzipped the hood, which was stowed inside the collar. He placed the jacket back on and pulled the hood up onto his head and did up the zipper at the front. He then walked back out of the restroom, took a last look back towards the front of the shop, placed his hands in his pockets and exited the shop via the rear delivery door. Devereaux moved quickly through the back of the complex and through a small hole in an old wooden picket fence that had seen better days. He glanced through a gap between two buildings and could see the white car parked across the road with the two occupants looking into the front of the shop.

He noticed a man wearing a heavy coat, get out of the white car from the passenger side and walk over to a payphone and proceeded to make a telephone call.

Devereaux walked further along the fence line, utilising its cover until he reached the street. Crossing the road, he made his way to a stairway that led down onto the platform of the Laverton Train Station. He checked his wallet for some change and purchased a ticket from the vending machine and then walked along the platform to take a seat and wait for the train.

He could see the blue car still parked as well as its occupants still sitting in the vehicle.

The train pulled up alongside the platform, and the doors opened. People started to board the train, barely giving off-loading passengers time to exit the carriage before they pushed their way on-board like storm troopers, with Devereaux merging into the centre of the chaos.

Positioning himself in an aisle seat and facing rearward, he had depth from view, making it harder for him to be seen and so that he could observe the surveilling parties as the train departed.

The train pulled away from the platform and rapidly built up speed. He had slipped them this time and felt quite pleased with himself. Nevertheless, they were amateurs, he thought to himself and knew that if they were well versed in the art of surveillance, the story would be very different.

These guys were from the Island, students, he thought to himself. The Island was the common name for ASIS's training centre for Intelligence Officers (IO's). Devereaux had been posted there as the 2IC of the Special Warfare Detachment and specialised in covert operations overseas. He pondered the rationale behind surveillance being placed on him. Who were they, and why was it important enough to put a tag on me? He questioned.

The only thing he could think of was that Connor was using the opportunity as another training exercise for his IO course. After passing numerous stations, a voice echoed over the carriage PA system, 'Next stop, Flinders Street Station'.

A sense of seriousness enveloped his demeanour as he continued to ponder why he had a tail. Was the Service keeping tabs on him to check out if he was suitable for the task that lay ahead? All these questions and more raced through his head.

If they were some trainees, then I'll just take full advantage of the situation and use it to my advantage... either way, I need to stay alert, he thought to himself as his eyes began scanning his surroundings.

Devereaux looked up as the train slowed and came to a halt alongside the platform. He waited until he could see which doorway would have the most people disembarking and quickly made his way to it, blending into the centre of the group. The doors slid open, and the crowd moved out onto the platform like sheep to a watering trough, pushing and bumping their way out until everyone had their own space. He merged with the heard until midway along the platform, then peeled off from the group into a side exit leading out of the station and on to a taxi rank. Devereaux surveyed the area, looking left and right, and noticed a tram stop about 75m from where he was.

Several people were standing in line waiting for the tram to arrive, all glum and pissed off because of the rain.

Pulling the hood back over his head, he made his way across the busy street and joined the queue and waited for the tram. The rain had started to ease, but a fine drizzle continued to fall.

Rolling his shoulders up and forwards, Devereaux placed his hands inside the pockets of his jacket as the wind sent a cold chill across the city.

'What a shit hole', he said to himself.

He never really cared for Melbourne, although, he enjoyed the multi-cultural aspect of its population, a fact that made the city rather interesting, if only for a short visit. But it was the weather he really hated, always drizzling or raining. At least that's how it seemed to him.

The green and yellow tram slowed to a halt and the queue filed on like well-disciplined troops. He decided to stand rather than to sit. This would make it harder for a surveillance team to acquire him, should, by chance, they get lucky.

The soft drone of the tram's electric engine began to fade as Irish music permeated the air. It steadily increased in volume until Devereaux bent over and glanced out the window and saw a large sign with green gothic fonts, which read, 'The Shamrock Inn'. Most eyes on the tram were drawn to the Shamrock as it passed by slowly, all peering to see why the music was so loud at this time of the morning. The tram accelerated once again, and the music faded as the tram made a right turn and headed down towards Elizabeth Street.

The tram came to a halt, and Devereaux stepped down and onto the roadway. Looking left and right, he briskly crossed the road between oncoming cars and then stepped up onto the pavement.

He looked up at a street sign, 'Little Bourke Street'.

Chinatown, excellent, he thought to himself. He had been down these streets a hundred times and knew the main exit and entry points available to him if he should need one of them to break contact.

As he made his way up the street, he saw an arcade that leads through to Bourke Street, and from there, the Southern Cross wasn't too far away.

Turning into Exhibition Street, Devereaux noticed the blue Ford pull up on the opposite side of the road, about 100 metres from his location.

He sidestepped into a small café and sat a meter or so back from the window so that he could observe while still having some depth from view. From here, he could see the vehicle and its passenger rather well.

'What can I get for you today' a soft voice asked.

'Just a cappuccino, please' he replied. The young girl scrawled something seemingly illegible onto the pad and turned and walked back to the counter. Devereaux watched as a female exited the car, wearing a light blue hoodie, denim jeans and sneakers.

She made her way over to a newsstand and purchased a paper and stood leaning against a fence.

She opened the paper and actioned as though she was reading it. From that location, she could observe the street all the way up to the front entrance of the hotel.

Her eyes were hard at work as she scoured the area for her quarry.

The blue Laser had moved off, continuing up the hill and past the entrance to the hotel. As it disappeared from sight, Devereaux assumed the vehicle had stopped on the other side of the crest so that the occupant could observe the other direction.

'Your cappuccino, sir' the tiny voice said.

Devereaux looked up at her face and saw a young woman, possibly 18 years of age, with the most charming smile. 'Thank you' he said with a smile and turned back to the window. Sipping his coffee, he remembered the "coffee" at the roadhouse on the way here and thought that there was just no comparison as he clutched the cup to warm his hands.

The rain started to come down more substantially, and the woman moved away from her vantage point to seek refuge under an awning.

'Perfect' Devereaux said to himself.

'That's right darling, allow yourself to feel uncomfortable and lose your concentration' he muttered.

Devereaux placed $5 on the table and exited the café. By now, the rain had really started to fall, and the awning where the woman had taken shelter had filled to capacity with others wanting to escape the downpour.

'Melbourne, you're not so bad, after all' he said to himself.

Devereaux ran a few metres and turned right into an alleyway and continued until he reached a fire escape.

On the third floor, he could see a door had been jammed open with a waste paper bin.

He scurried up the ladder and entered the building, making his way to the central stairs. The building was turn-of-the-century and had seen better days. The stairs were made of old Jarrah timber with a deep red finish. The carpet was old, paisley in pattern and in reasonable condition.

Devereaux moved towards a window on the second floor and cautiously peered out. The window was directly across from the hotel, and he could see a man who was a passenger in the white Laser standing on the corner. To the right was the rear entrance to the hotel.

Devereaux could see that there was good cover and figured that he would be able to use the cover of numerous vehicles entering and exiting the hotel service bay area, blocking the view of the surveillance team.

Continuing down the stairs and out the entrance, Devereaux carefully peered around the corner and observed the man. He was looking up towards the main entrance as Devereaux used the cover of a truck to make his dash across the street and into the service entrance of the hotel.

Moving through the basement area of the hotel, he turned into a corridor and came face-to-face with a hotel security guard.

'Can I help you, sir?' the huge bulk of a man asked.

'Yes, excuse me for taking this entrance, but as you can see from my clothes, I'm half-drowned from the terrible weather outside – so I decided to take a short cut rather than to continue in the deluge'.

'Well, sir, this is a restricted area, and you must use the main entrance' the man said.

'I know you're right, but I'm meeting a very important client here for lunch, and as you can see, I would be totally soaked if I hadn't taken this route' Devereaux replied.

The man looked at him, 'if you don't mind me saying so, sir, you look like shit!' he said with a warm smile.

'Take the lift to the lobby, it's just around the corner to your right', he added.

'Thanks, I really appreciate it!' Devereaux said and made his way to the lift.

The lift door opened, and he stepped in. Pushing the button for the lobby, the lift began to move upward before finally came to a halt. The doors opened, and Devereaux scanned the lobby for the surveillance team. To the left, he could see Connor sitting in the almost deserted Lobby Café drinking what looked to be a café latté, judging by the height of the glass. He had a newspaper opened – 'The Financial Review' – and seemed to be intent on reading.

He noticed that Connor had chosen a table away from the window as well as the mainstream traffic that would come and go from the café. To the right, he saw the young woman who had taken shelter from the rain talking to another man whom Devereaux hadn't yet picked up on. Both had their attention drawn to another area as Devereaux made his way over to Connor. Without looking up, Connor said, 'You sly dog! Although I thought you would have been here at least an hour ago.'

'Sorry to disappoint you, old son, but I had a bit of shopping to do and was badly in need of a pedicure' he retorted.

Devereaux looked over at the woman as she glanced up and spotted him next to Connor. Her disappointment was evident as she exhaled in disbelief, her eyes widened, and her shoulders drooped with the heavy burden of defeat. She tapped her male companion on the arm and gestured with her eyes for him to look in that direction.

Devereaux gave a gentle nod and slight wave while his hunters feigned a smile and returned his wave.

'Well, a few hundred more of those exercises and they should be ready for Ops – don't you think?' Devereaux suggested.

'I think you made your point with them. Glad to see you could make it John, and even more so that your humour is still intact,' Connor was quick to add.

'The Director will be ready for us in about an hour, so I thought it might be a good opportunity for me to get you up to speed on the current situation leading up to our decision to mount this operation' he said.

'Since 1981, we have been monitoring the Thai Government's protection of Pol Pot at a camp in the south-eastern sector of Thailand, along the Thai-Cambodian border.

Discussions with the Thai Government behind closed doors have failed to have them hand him over to be tried by an international court in The Hague. The U.S. has demonstrated a fence-sitting posture and has not been willing to apply pressure on the Thai Government, as it needs them on side for regional security reasons.'

'On the other hand, the Thais maintain protective operations of Pol Pot, we believe to maintain a soft instability in Cambodia, creating a buffer between its perceived enemy, Vietnam' he continued. 'It seems old animosities die hard in this neck of the woods' he added.

'Bush and Keating have been having serious discussions about the dilemma and agree that it is imperative that we move to stabilise the country before we send in a peacekeeping force to establish fair elections and return to an orderly society - if that is even possible' he said.

Devereaux looked confused.

'So, you want me to wander into Cambodia and pave the way for your elections?' he said with some fascination.

'Not quite, old son' Connor replied.

'The issue at hand is not Pol Pot – he won't last much longer anyway - word has it that he's seriously ill. But we have intercepted information relating to the redistribution of weapons that will be collected during the demobilisation of forces before the election'.

'A vast quantity of weapons is to be collected and destroyed. We believe, however, based on the information at hand that a large portion of the weapons will never make the melting pot' Connor added.

He continued, 'We believe an operation is being planned, and or in the early stages of execution, to filter off the best of the weapons and then redistribute those weapons to the highest bidder. What's of interest to us, and will be to you, too, is that the Thai Government has assigned General Getti with the task of coordinating the disarmament of factions and destroying the weapons.'

'But we have reason to believe that Getti himself is heavily involved, if not the real mastermind, behind the operation to filter off the weapons.

We know, thanks to various sources, that he intends to offer them to the Karen guerrillas on the Burmese border' he added.

Devereaux continued to listen intently as Connor paused to beckon a waitress over to their secluded location in the café.

Devereaux looked over his shoulder as the waitress approached and said, 'I'd love a pot of tea, please – maybe English Breakfast, if you don't mind?'

'Yes, sir, we have it – and you, sir, what would you like?' she said as she turned towards Connor.

'Long Black, please' he said. The waitress turned and made her way back to the bar as the two men resumed their discussion.

'I don't need to tell you what this means to the peace process, not to mention the elections. All our efforts to bring peace to Cambodia will be wasted, and the world is watching, mate. So, we had better prevent this from ever happening, or the elections may very well be dead before they even start – and Australia will look like utter fools.'

Devereaux looked around as the waitress approached and delivered the order.

'That will be $8.00 please, sir' the waitress said. Connor placed a $10 note on her tray, and the girl moved off once again, thanking him with just a silent nod.

'Ok Connor, what is the assignment, and when do we commence the operation?' Devereaux asked somewhat impatiently.

'The operation has already commenced to some extent' he replied. 'But I will leave that to Webb to fill you in on that information. He's ready to see us now, so let's head upstairs and start, shall we?' Connor said as he finished off the last of his coffee.

Devereaux hurried down his tea, stood and followed Connor through the lobby to the lift.

CHAPTER 6

'Brimstone'

SOUTHERN CROSS HOTEL

11:00hrs

Connor removed a plastic key card to Suite 20-06 and slid the card into the slot, pushing the card down to complete the circuit. Two green lights illuminated to permit access. He pushed the door open and walked into the suite. Devereaux took one last glance down the hallway, noting the two emergency exit stairways, then followed behind Connor.

The suite was enormous and well-appointed, albeit dated – not of antiquity, but a more modern era, perhaps from the early to mid-'70s. The carpets were white in colour and of a mild-shag cut.

The walls were a cream colour that had white timber borders and cornice trimming on the ceiling, which caught the light and gave a sense of the room's size.

Massive floor to ceiling French windows poured natural light into the room while heavy, gold-coloured curtains hung at the end of each curtain rail. The master bedroom was off to the left, and a large sitting area was to the right, furnished with two large, dark brown leather Chesterfield sofas and two matching leather chairs. In the corner was a well-stocked bar.

Devereaux looked across the room. A lone, silhouetted figure stood at the window, peering out at the city below, the windowpanes covered in droplets of rain, some trickling down and leaving tracks of clarity.

The motionless figure at the window stood tall at about 183cm and had black hair that was greying heavily on the sides.

One hand was in his pocket, the other parting the sheer white curtain with an index finger as he peered outside. His well-tailored dark grey suit emanated quality – Savile Row, perhaps, Devereaux thought.

A voice from the figure rang out across the stillroom.

'Take a seat, gentlemen,' and Director-General Magnus Webb turned to make eye contact and forced a smile of welcome.

'Magnus, this is John Devereaux.'

'John, this is Director-General of ASIS, Magnus Webb.'

'Nice to meet you, sir' Devereaux replied and reached out and shook Webb's hand.

'Nice to meet you too. I've heard good things about you, John', Magnus replied.

Connor made his way across to a Chesterfield chair, one with a high back and deeply studded buttons, while Devereaux took a seat on the leather sofa.

'Coffee or Tea, gentlemen?' Webb asked

'Tea, thank you' Devereaux replied.

'I'll just help myself to the bar' said Connor.

Webb glanced over at Devereaux with a smile and then raised his eyebrows.

'Some things never change, Connor' said, Webb.

Connor, standing at the bar with his back turned, raised his left hand as if to wave acknowledgement, then returned across the room to his seat, a tumbler glass of whisky and ice in his hand.

'I understand Connor has briefed you on the current plan and the purpose of our discussion? My role here, John, is to formally task you with a mission, in a rather, how shall we phrase it... "Unofficial Manner".

The task at hand is one we see as imperative for the success of the UNTAC mission commencing in January of next year' Webb added.

'Australia must be seen on the international stage as being competent in managing issues of great importance in the region, and we must remove every obstacle that may prevent our success' Webb said, and then took a sip of his coffee.

'For the purpose of this mission, you have been seconded to ASIS until further notice. The mission you are about to embark on is code name: "BRIMSTONE." Your mission is to terminate General Sompon Getti at the earliest possible opportunity', Webb added. 'As you were aware, you were only partially successful last time."

Looking directly into Webb's eyes, Devereaux said... 'I thought it was a major success on my part. The only fuck up was the intelligence I received from you clowns that proved to be incorrect.' Devereaux's piercing gaze continued.

Connor looked over towards the window, a slight smile etched on his face, finding Devereaux's remark amusing, particularly because he knew Webb had never had a subordinate that spoke his mind, well, at least not one that spoke so directly.

After an unintended pause from Webb, somewhat surprised at the remark's cutting edge, Webb looked across at Connor and smiled... 'I think I'm going to like him.' he responded.

Turning back to Devereaux, Webb continued.

'Your point is well taken John, and I was not having a go at you. I was simply stating the fact that the purpose of that mission under former DG Stevens was not fully achieved, for whatever reason.'

'In fact, in the end, and on a positive note, it served a greater purpose in that Pim's people think it was Getti that had Pim terminated, which has now seen some infighting between the two camps. As a result, Getti's business has struggled over the past 12 months.'

'Getti is determined to rectify this, and as such, we have uncovered information that Getti plans to take control of the decommissioned weapons from the KR before they are destroyed. He plans to resell them the black market after UNTAC is complete- of course, the purpose of this is to keep the western area of Cambodia somewhat lawless, which would benefit his private operations. Besides, we understand that he plans to provide weapons to the Karen on the Thai-Burma border. Getti is also heavily involved in the growing of poppies and the manufacture of heroin. The distribution element of his business is second-to-none and has been exporting heroin to several western countries, including that of Australia since February 1989. He stands to make a considerable amount of money and gain additional power from his operations, and we can't allow this to happen' Webb insisted.

'You see, John, Getti is somewhat of a bad apple, but very well connected within the Thai Government and within the Thai Royal Family. He is a 'protected species', so to speak'. With that in mind, you are tasked with an executive action mission to terminate Getti at the earliest possible opportunity by a means and location of your own choosing' Webb ordered.

Devereaux looked intently at Webb, then at Connor.

'So... this is an off the books sanction, right?'

'John' Webb said, 'you are assigned this task as a Non-Official Cover (NOC) operative and will receive deep cover support in the sphere of intelligence, funding and equipment. If something goes pear-shaped, however, you will be disavowed for obvious reasons' Webb replied. Devereaux looked across the room and back at Webb and nodded his head indicating he understood what had just been served up to him, but equally aware his question as to the mission being "Off the Books" was deliberately sidestepped.

'John, it's no accident that you were chosen, and no offence, but you are not what I would call the "Special Forces" stereotype. I mean, to look at you, you are not overly buff or muscular, you are of average height at 180cm, you are in your 40s, and you don't fit that image, at least not the image that would make people notice you' he added. 'Again, no offence intended', he continued.

'None taken' Devereaux replied.

'Your demeanour reflects mediocracy – the average Joe Blow, so to speak. And as insulting as that may sound, it's precisely why you are a most valued operative and have been chosen for this mission. Of course, your tradecraft has proven to be second-to-none' Webb said.

'You know how the service works, John, and you understand its intonation' Connor added.

'You will be in plain sight, John, and they won't even see you coming' Webb said.

'Connor, I will have that whiskey now, thanks' Devereaux exclaimed.

Standing and walking over to the window, Devereaux looked out and watched the populace below scurry around dodging the rain. It seemed to be getting heavier as the day went on, Devereaux thought to himself. Maybe that was an ominous sign given the mission at hand.

Connor passed a tumbler to Devereaux, and he took a small sip. 'Thanks' he said.

'I take it we have a budget for this operation?' Devereaux asked.

'It's not endless, John, but given the need, it's quite substantial. What do you need?' replied Webb.

'I will need several different passports that can be validated, of course – one Australian, one U.S. and one U.K. should just about do it.

I'll also need cash in U.S. dollars and Thai baht. I'll let you know the exact amount later.

There will also be equipment requirements, so once I have time to digest the mission's needs, I will get back to you.'

'No, we will not be seeing each other after this meeting. You will be reporting directly to Connor and Connor alone' Webb said. 'Get a list of whatever you need and give it to Connor; he will make sure you get it.'

Webb stood closer to Devereaux, extended his hand and said, 'good luck Devereaux, we're counting on your success'. Turning towards Connor, Webb said, 'feel free to stay and use the suite – I know you will help yourself to my whiskey.'

'It's booked until tomorrow morning at 10am', Webb said, permitting himself a cheeky smile as he collected his overcoat and umbrella and made his way to the door.

Draining the last of his whiskey from his tumbler, Connor replied, 'I'll stay in contact, usual means.'

Without turning toward Connor, or muttering a single word, Webb raised the umbrella that he clutched in his left hand as if to acknowledge him, and then exited the suite allowing the door to close behind him. With that, Webb was gone. The assignment was handed to Devereaux as if it were just another day at the office.

Devereaux stood glancing out of the window while Connor sat in the armchair.

'So, your thoughts, ol' boy?' Connor asked.

Devereaux, still content looking out at the scurrying people below, paused for a few seconds and then said, 'thoughts?'

'Yes, Connor, I have a myriad of thoughts bouncing around my skull at the moment' he said.

'What Safe Houses do we have operational in Bangkok?' Devereaux asked.

'I maintain a safe house in Sukhumvit and one outside of Bangkok, down in Hua Hin' Connor replied. 'Both are fully stocked with escape and evasion grab bags as well as communications – you know the usual stuff.'

Devereaux walked away from the window and sat back down on the sofa. Connor looked over at John, acutely aware of the current situation at the Devereaux household.

'How's Alesha and the kids?' Connor asked.

Devereaux looked at his watch and then turned to Connor.

'Well, they should be landing in Perth right about now' he said.

'Is this something that is going to caused difficulties for you at this time?' Connor asked with some empathy.

Devereaux pondered the question and then took a sip of his whisky. 'It's been a long-time coming Anthony.

I am surprised the marriage lasted this long; however, it did, and yes, it's a tough one at the moment but not unexpected. It may in time be the best thing' Devereaux responded. 'So, if you are wondering if I am up to this the mission, the answer is yes, and in fact, it's just what I need right now' he added.

CHAPTER 7

'Kozlov'

MOSCOW

Grey clouds saturated the sky above, their reflection mirrored on the rainwater-covered roads below. The power lines suspended overhead dripped with water, while other water droplets were still frozen in time along the same lines. Beside the verge of the road, remnants of a late winter fall built up a mound of dirty snow. People in heavy coats walked along the sidewalk, taking each step with care to avoid the thin layer of ice embedded into the concrete underfoot. The ornately designed buildings of a different era along Strada Ilyinka created a concrete canyon in the metropolis of Moscow.

On top of the southeast corner of the GUM Shopping Mall was a privately-owned office overlooking Red Square, the Kremlin and St. Basil's Cathedral. Vladimir Kozlov sat behind a massive oak desk, that was adorned with intricately carved woodwork.

The carvings in the timber were exquisite, gold gilding inlays were set to testify to its owner's wealth. The desk was like that of the Resolute Desk in the Oval Office, something that Kozlov thought was befitting of himself and his global criminal empire. Affixed to the wall directly behind the desk in a heavy, gold-gilded frame, hung an opulent portrait of the Theotokos of Vladimir – the Orthodox icon depicting Christ the child snuggling into the cheek of the Mother Mary.

The portrait was strategically positioned overlooking the desk and, thus, the "enterprise," in order to act as a guardian from misfortune and misery.

The walls of the office had gold-wallpapered panels bordered by massive timber beams. Subtle wall-mounted chandeliers were affixed to the centre of each wallpaper panel, and around the walls were built-in sofas with plush scarlet upholstery with deep studded buttons.

A man sat on the sofa to the left of the door reading the "Komsomolskaya Pravda" newspaper, his long black oily hair pulled back in a ponytail, his shiny black designer silk suit symbolising his rise to success and the tell-tale tattoos signifying his violent past. Next to him on the sofa was a Heckler and Koch MP-5 "K" model submachine gun. A second man stood behind the bar cleaning wine glasses, a scar running from the corner of his mouth up to his right earlobe, a reminder of a razor's edge. His baldhead heavily tattooed with prison art, next to him on the bar, a Glock 26 pistol. Both men were over 185cm tall and both were heavyset… they were the muscle.

Vladimir Kozlov sat behind the desk; his black Armani suit immaculate. To his right, a Glock-19 pistol rested on the desk next to a set of car keys, the Mercedes Benz emblem clearly visible. He reached out with his left hand, grasping the neck of the "Legend of Kremlin" vodka bottle and poured some of the finest Russian Vodka available into a tumbler glass.

On the back of his hand, a rising sun tattoo with the letters "CEBEP" below indicating that he had been imprisoned in a northern corrections facility.

On his left ring finger was a tattoo of the Saint Petersburg Cross, showing that Kozlov had also been incarcerated in Saint Petersburg – Kresty Prison.

Five black dots just below his left thumb signified a five-year prison term. He was a hardened criminal, the boss of Moscow's

Solntsevskaya organised crime gang. He was also Vory V Zakone - the "Thieves–In-Law", the Russian mafia, and he maintained rule with an iron fist. He gained following by emphasising loyalty above all else to each other and total resistance to the government authorities – he was a true Vor.

As he sipped Vodka from the crystal tumbler, his mind pondering the business day ahead, the large timber floor to ceiling doors to his office opened. Walking in with a sense of urgency was Sergei Pushkin, Kozlov's grandson.

'Dedushka...' Sergei called to his Grandfather.

'What is it, Sergei?'

'They have destroyed our shipment in Koshk, Afghanistan, just short of the border. We lost 500kgs' he replied.

Kozlov stared at Sergei, the veins in his forehead begging to explode, his teeth ready to crumble under pressure exerted upon them. He turned in his chair, throwing the crystal tumbler across the room and smashing the glass on the corner of the bar.

'Fuck!' yelled Kozlov. 'When did this happen and who is responsible?'

'The information I have, Dedushka, is that the shipment was attacked at 9pm last night. We believe it was taken and burned by the Mujahidin,' Sergei responded.

'Burned? … bullshit. Those motherfuckers wouldn't burn it – they will on-sell it, Sergei' barked the Dedushka, his eyes looking at Sergei in disbelief that a grandson of his could be so naïve.

'They have arrested Safi just short of the border, but he knows nothing except for the delivery site location in Turkmenistan' he added.

'What the hell was Safi doing delivering the shipment? Safi will no doubt be dead by now.'

'500kgs, fuck!' Kozlov muttered. 'This fucks our supply lines up for the foreseeable future, at least from Central Asia.' Kozlov said.

'We need to contact the Thais and see what we can arrange as an interim supply line. Where is Drozdov at the moment?' he asked.

'He will be arriving in Marseille at 2pm today' Sergei responded quickly.

'He needs to go to Thailand as soon as possible' Kozlov said as he thought through the ramifications of the loss of his supply from Afghanistan.

The bald-headed man walked over and placed another crystal tumbler on the desk, lifted the bottle and poured another shot into the tumbler. Then, in one fluid motion, slid the glass across to Kozlov, who looked up at the bald-headed man and raised his eyebrows in a gesture of thanks. The bald man nodded in a sign of acknowledgement, before returning to the area of the bar and cleaning up the broken glass.

'Sergei... book me a flight to Monaco for tomorrow morning' Kozlov commanded.

'Get in touch with Drozdov and tell him to meet me at the "Coco Cubano" tomorrow at 6pm.'

MONACO

The 70m-pleasure yacht, the "Coco Cubano", was moored in its pen on Quai Rainier 1er in Port Hercules, Monaco. On its stern, the Cayman Islands flag swayed gently in the light breeze.

Kozlov had the Italian shipyard Belletti make the majestic steel and aluminium vessel. The Coco Cubano accommodated up to 20 guests in 10 palatial cabins, with the master cabin more akin to a presidential suite where gold was the main feature throughout the room. A gold-plated elevator connected all the decks. No expense had been spared.

The vessel's main saloon boasted a large dining area where a hand-carved dining table that seated 20 was adorned with an impressive selection of Versace crockery.

One deck up was the sky lounge with a fully equipped bar, cinema screen and seating were on plush leather sofas arranged in a semi-circle facing the rear of the vessel.

The Coco Cubano was evidence that the Russian mafia's illicit dealing was doing well... very well indeed!

Kozlov sat at the stern on the sky lounge deck overlooking the saloon and main decks below; the lights of Monaco glistened as the remaining sunlight departed the skies above. Sitting either side of Kozlov were two beautiful, blonde Ukrainian women drinking champagne. On the deck and to the rear of the sky lounge were two-armed security guards. The deck below, another two guards.

Like a panther moving silently, a black Mercedes Benz S500 purred along the pier below, stopping just short of the gangway. The purr of the engine came to a halt as the S500's ignition was switched off.

The driver's door opened, and a Hugo Boss, black leather Oxford shoe came in contact with the ground. His grey Savile Row suit was impeccable, tailored perfectly for him in Mayfair, London.

Under his blazer, he wore a white silk T-Shirt.

The short-haired blonde man stood at 185cm, he was well built and was very fit.

He was in his early 40's and had piercing blue eyes, which hinted that he was most likely from the Saint Petersburg or Vyborg regions. The delineation between the blonde man and Kozlov was that the blonde man bore no tattoos; instead, he was a former KGB officer - Aleksandr Drozdov, had arrived.

'Aleksandr, good to see you, my friend' said Kozlov.

Drozdov made his way across to the sofa and sat down.

'Good to see you to boss' came the reply in a polished Russian accent. 'But what was the rush? I just landed in Marseille and got your message to meet you here... is everything ok?'

'Ladies... go for a walk, I have some business to take care of' Kozlov said to the two Ukrainian blondes.

After the women had left, Kozlov moved across to the bar and poured to straight vodkas and walked across to Drozdov and passed him one of the drinks.

'Yes, actually, we have a major supply problem emanating out of Afghanistan. Those fucking Mujahidin ragheads highjacked our mules just short of the border.

500kg stolen from me - from me' he shouted. 'I'm going to send those fucks a message.' Kozlov said in guttural Russian that was more befitting his mood than his education. During times of anger, Kozlov often descended into an animal-like state - heaven help anyone who crossed him or got in his way. Drozdov looked intently at his Vodka, knowing what that meant for his operation on the French Riviera. Looking back up at Kozlov he said...

'Well then, that has to be a very loud message so there can be no future misunderstandings.'

'I have two tasks for you' said Vladimir. 'Use your connections at the SVR to find out who is the most likely group to jack our shipment. Then put the word out that we have organised another shipment of 1000kg and that it is being moved along the same route. I want the truck to be one fucking big VBIED.' Kozlov added.

'Make sure that it detonates so that it causes maximum casualties. It has to be a big fucking explosion Aleksandr; I want them to know they can't fuck with us. So, get onto it and make it happen.'

Drozdov drank the last of his Vodka and placed the tumbler onto the table in front of him.

'As for making it a big message, I wouldn't have it any other way. It will cost a bit to pay off the right people, but it's as good as done.'

'Now, as for the second task?' he asked.

'Yes, the second task. I want you in Thailand this week to organise a replacement shipment for the 500kg we just lost. Set up an amicable deal for the short to mid-term.

Who knows how long it will be before our supplies from those fucking ragheads recommences?' Kozlov said with an air of resentment.

Drozdov knew precisely what he meant. Any delays in supply would undoubtedly see rivals' step in and take over the business, and that would not be permissible as once the ground is lost, it has to be taken back again and nobody wanted to see, or indeed had the stomach for a turf war.

CHAPTER 8

'Powder'

MAE HONG SONG, THAILAND

The old woman sat stirring raw opium in a large metal vat using an oar like wooden paddle. The vat sat over the heat of a wood fire, and as she churned the opium, steam formed and rose upwards removed the water content from the opium. Her hair was tied back with a piece of beige coloured cheesecloth that had seen better days, and her weathered face was creviced with wrinkles that belied her age of 55 years. With her teeth blackened by the opium pipe, she looked closer to 70.

It was so hot that sweat fell from the old woman's forehead as she toiled under the thatch roof hut.

As she stopped to wipe her brow with her forearm, she saw in the distance, a line of people heading towards the village, some on foot, and others on horseback.

They broke through the jungle tree line and made their way towards the village on a brown, dusty earth track that separated two large poppy fields.

On either side of the poppy fields, large, steep limestone karsts locked the location away from the rest of the world. It was a Shangri-La of sorts, a hidden oasis where the growing of opium and the manufacture of heroin could be done at will.

There was only one entry to the canyon, a seemingly impenetrable environment – and, along the way, lookout posts secreted in limestone caves that were invisible to those below. The heavily armed sentries in the caves provided overwatch of the route to the village. The sentries giving the village warning of visitors long before they even reached the Shangri-La.

The track to the village was on narrow footpads that were at times, very steep, making it difficult for the horses to negotiate. The jungle was thick, with a dense primary canopy and an abundant secondary growth made movement difficult. At times visibility at ground level was only a few metres.

As the men and women approached the village, the white and pink carpet of blooming poppies flanked them on either side. Workers tending the poppy fields, dressed in dark blue pyjama-like clothing and wore large straw brimmed hats to protect them from the relentless, blistering sun, stopped what they were doing and looked up at the visitors as they trod the dirt track.

Still 500m from the village, a man of stature and riding on horseback, raised his hand and called out, 'Yut', and the riders and those walking all came to a halt.

General Sompon Getti climbed down off of his horse, and a man on foot came and took hold of the reigns as Getti told him to continue to the village. The rest of the caravan moved forward on foot, their beasts of burden enjoying a well-earned rest.

Getti and another man, a young man in his late twenties, walked through the poppy field to inspect the crop and talk to the farmers. Each farmer was asked not how the crop was, but how his family was doing. Each farmer tending the crop was then given 2,000 Baht, and every one of them grabbed the hand of the General and thanked him profusely.

Every worker in the village that day would receive 2,000 Baht, as the General had learned that keeping the farmers happy would provide him with far higher yields and solidify their loyalty.

Chatri, General Getti's son, stood next to him wearing an olive drab army uniform, an M16 slung across his back, watching everything his father was doing as he learned and mastered the business.

Getti waded through the crop, checking the poppies as he passed, stopping now and again and inspecting the pod for maturity.

'Chatri, what is it about this opium poppy pod... is it ready to be scored?' asked his father.

Chatri took hold of the pod in his hand and looked carefully at it.

'Yes, father, this pod is mature and ready to be scored' the young Getti responded.

'How so?' asked the father.

Chatri took another look at the pod.

'You can tell, father, because the crown of each pod is standing out and are slightly curved upwards.'

'Is that so? What else tells you it is ready to score?'

'There is also a faint brown line on the bottom side of the pod,' Chatri answered.

Looking at his son with some pride, the General slapped him on the shoulder. No words were needed – his proud slap was enough.

'Ok, score the pod, son' said the General, as he passed the son a scoring knife.

'Make sure you score the pod in an upward direction to get the most yield.' The General directed his son.

Holding the Somniclaw, the three-bladed scoring knife, Chatri sliced into the skin of the pod.

'Chatri, score it from the bottom in an upwards motion – bottom to top' directed the General.

The obedient son complied, making another three incisions into the pod. After each incision, a white, latex-like raw opium oozed to the surface.

'So, tell me, my son, when can the product be harvested from the pod?'

'It will take another 24 hours, father before it has dried and turned to a brown colour. Then we can harvest it' said the son.

'What is the average yield of opium from each pod?'

'I'm unsure, father' Chatri replied.

'The average yield is 80 milligrams per pod. You need to know this for your production capacity, son' the father urged.

'So, from each hectare of poppies, we will harvest between eight and fifteen kilograms of opium.'

'Well done, you're learning fast' said the proud father.

The Karen tribal village was perched high in the mountains, 15km west of Mae Hong Song. The main building, and by far the largest, sat in the middle of the village. Its large A-framed roof, covered with grass thatching, was surrounded with smaller homes scattered in a circular pattern. The main building was the central processing and storage building, and everything fed into that structure – but each building in the centre cluster of the village had a purpose in the manufacturing cycle.

Getti walked around the buildings, looking at the processing taking place, pointing out the finer points of production to his son.

He was teaching him how to streamline production; how to motivate the workers, and how to ship the product from the village to the rest of the world - Chatri was being groomed to take over.

125

Getti approached the main building and saw the familiar face of the old lady as she stirred the opium in the vat.

Getti smiled at her, and she responded by nodding and smiling broadly, her blackened teeth not going unnoticed, but politely not mentioned.

The opium being boiled in the vat was a light brown colour, which indicated to Getti that the quality was excellent – too dark, and the quality would be inadequate.

'Chatri, take over from her and start stirring' said the General.

The good son did precisely what his father had told him. The others watched as the son worked the vat, knowing all too well that this was not a punishment or a demotion in stature, instead they knew Getti was teaching his son every aspect of the trade, which earned Chatri the highest respect of the villagers. Chatri stirred the opium in the vat as it boiled, the old woman correcting his technique as required – and each time she corrected him, he thanked her with honest respect.

The main building was almost entirely made of wood. The massive beams that held the thatched roof in place had been hand cut from the nearby forest. The walls were woven palm frond leaves, some tightly woven, others left with holes so that some air could pass through. The floor was entirely made from hand-sawn planks of teak, the planks 20cm wide. On the right side of the entrance were large, heavy pieces of furniture that had a Southern Chinese influence in the design. Some wooden stools were placed alongside tables that could seat 20 people. On this occasion, however, the tables were partially stacked with 1kg bricks of processed heroin, a distinctive Red Naga logo stamped on a white sticker that was affixed to the silver foil wrapping.

Getti's powder was 97-99% pure, a fact that made his heroin some of the very best in the world and a most sought-after product, particularly in the U.S., Europe and Australia.

'Chatri, come here son.'

'We produce a product that is in such high demand in Europe, the U.S. and Australia, that we have difficulty in supplying the volume, but while other lesser quality products are selling for US$100,000 to US$110,000 per kilogram on the street, ours is eventually sold for US$160,000 per kilogram. Never forget quality Chatri, maintain the purity levels and never take the easy way out,' he lectured his son.

The loyal son nodded in acknowledgement as he picked up a brick of powder.

'How many kilograms do we have here?' he asked.

'150kgs' responded Getti. Chatri paused, calculating the cost in his head and turned back to his father.

'That's US$22,500,000' he said, looking at his father in disbelief. For the first time, Chatri understood his father's business obsession.

'Yes, that's a lot of money, son, but our take on that is only 20%.' He said as he leaned forward and picked up a brick, his mind pondering the margins and how he could make that entitlement much larger.

'Still, that is US$4,500,000 from this farm alone. We have another five farms all producing a similar product and quantity,' the father turned and smiled.

'So, you can see the importance of learning this business, as you will eventually take everything over. Your current position in the government, albeit vitally important, is only a stepping stone to ensuring greater wealth and security for our family's future.' 'Son, we need to discuss the development of a plan that would see us securing a larger portion of the profits. If we supply directly to Europe, we may be able to double our profit at least.' He added.

Getti and his son walked around the production site. A car jack was ingeniously being used as a press to make the powder into solid bricks. A second woman was getting the next brick ready for compression by carefully weighing and pouring the powder into another wooden mould. At the other end of the building were eight more large steel vats boiling the opium to reduce the water content and turning the opium into a plasticine-type consistency. Next to the woman stirring the vats were several cane baskets, all were full of brown opium balls the size of small coconuts, waiting their turn in the vat. Leaning against the basket was the woman's AK-47. The AK had seen much better days as surface rust had started to form on the barrel and receiver housing.

The next morning, Getti and his team were preparing to leave – and, with them, 150kgs of high-grade heroin.

Four men were busy packing the bricks into hessian bags and lashing them onto the harness on the horses. Getti and Chatri walked around the village saying goodbye and thanking the villagers for all of their hard work.

As they walked back along the dirt track that they came in on, Getti turned to his son.

'Chatri, what was the most important thing you learned here?' Chatri looked around the village and the poppy fields. There was silence for a few seconds as Chatri considered the question.

'I think the process, father. The need to maintain high quality at each step of the process' he responded.

'Certainly, that is true. However, what I wanted you to take away from this whole exercise son, is the importance of your people. On arrival, we went out of our way to greet them individually, the last thing we did was to go and see them personally and say goodbye.'

'You need to show them they are important to you. You do that, son, and you will always remain on top,' the father advised his son.

'In a month's time, this site will have another 200kgs ready,' the General said with a smile.

Business was good!

CHAPTER 9

'The Annex'

THE ISLAND, VICTORIA

05:30hrs

The night had passed by slowly, with only a few hours of unbroken sleep, Devereaux woke feeling quite shattered. He sat up in the bed and felt the silence around him. The house on Santa Monica Boulevard in Point Lonsdale was silent and empty. No signs of life stirred as Alesha and the kids had gone back to Perth. Their return was something Devereaux and Alesha had not discussed, at least in any depth. Devereaux flopped back on the bed, his head on the pillow as the sense of loss weighed heavily on his mind. Both had reservations as to the longevity of the marriage, and it seemed that the numbness that had permeated between them was finally starting to solidify – the end was not too far away.

Devereaux was not surprised. Not many women can last the distance of having their husband away for nine months a year.

Always leaving at a moment's notice, the sounds of a pager piercing the night's silence - a grab bag always packed and ready to go - a kiss on her forehead as she slept - a silent goodbye.

Hell, who would blame her? Devereaux certainly didn't. SAS life was so unpredictable, so severe, and so unforgiving.

The churning of coffee beans being ground and the hiss of steam from the coffee machine produced a welcoming odour in the house as Devereaux made his first caffeine hit of the day.

He had not slept well last night, his mind on Magnus Webb and the nonchalant manner of delivering the mission. A high-profile target such as Getti surely warranted far more respect, and indeed, one would expect, a far more detailed briefing from the Director-General of ASIS.

It seemed that Webb was eager to deliver the mission and depart at the earliest possible moment, severing ties to the deed that followed. That positively reeked of a very hands-off approach, a fact that Devereaux would have to be mindful of.

As a NOC, he was aware that he had limited support and would never be acknowledged should the shit hit the fan. It was like he had open slather to complete the task at hand - no questions asked. Sometimes, things make the hairs on the back of your neck stand up... and the hairs on the back of Devereaux's neck were indeed at attention.

The dark blue 1989 Volvo 740 slowed and came to a halt at the security checkpoint at the entry to the Island. The guard, manning the post, a grey-haired man in his late 60's, was wearing a maroon cardigan. He glanced up and looked over the top of his glasses and nodded his head, then reached down and pressed the red access button bringing life into the boom gate.

Devereaux nodded and proceeded through the gate, continuing across the one-lane bridge onto the Island and turned right towards the second security point.

Reaching into the top pocket of his shirt, he removed a blank white card, then reached out of the open window towards a silver metal post and swiped the card against the black-coloured scanner. A buzzing noise could be heard as two gates located on the 3m high cyclone fence began to open.

Moving the gear lever into drive, he edged forward and through the opening and stopped again about 10m on the other side. Devereaux looked into the rearview mirror and waited for the gates to close once again before driving on. Weaving his way along the narrow winding asphalt road, lined on either side with an almost impenetrable barrier of coastal brush bushes, he slowed his vehicle to 20kms per hour to allow 3 runners to pass by. The lead runner he noticed was Rachel, the other woman running with her was the woman seeking shelter from the rain in Melbourne, and from the failed surveillance team. The third runner, a male, was someone he had not seen before – they were trainees from the Intelligence Officer course.

Devereaux looked in the rear vision mirror as they passed by, noticing as Rachel turned her head and watched the passing vehicle, no doubt recognising Devereaux, the arrogant, demanding agent, she picked up a few nights before.

Slowing his car at the third security point, he reached out of the window and pressed a black button on the intercom. He looked up at the camera, and within a few seconds, he heard a metallic click as the gate locks opened. Driving through and following the procedure at the second checkpoint, Devereaux stopped and waited for the gate to close before driving off. He followed the road to the right passing some old 1950's buildings; old houses that had been converted into classrooms and briefing facilities, some old warehouse buildings used for training and storage of equipment and a fleet of cars.

On the right, he pulled into a car park behind an old brick structure that was built in the late 1950s and acted as the main administrative building as well as housing most of the lecture rooms.

Entering through some double doors, Devereaux could see Connor in the Mess making some coffee.

'Just in time, ol' son – care for a coffee?' Connor asked.

'Love one, mate' Devereaux replied.

'White with one, right?'

'Yes mate, that's perfect.'

'How'd you sleep?' Connor asked.

'Like a baby' Devereaux said, lying through his teeth; the bags under his eyes must have been a dead giveaway.

Connor handed Devereaux his coffee.

'Thanks mate' He replied.

'Walk with me, John' Connor said, and the pair exited the building and walked along the road towards the Annex, an old house reserved for people they wished to keep out of view from others on the Island. The Annex would be the perfect place to hold their discussion without fear of compromise.

The Annex was an old house made of fibro and had an old corrugated tin roof. It was surrounded by a three-meter high hedge, making the building mostly invisible to prying eyes.

Connor walked up to the front door, leaned forward and placed his eye against the eye scanner, and pressed the 'scan' button. A green light flashed, and the sound of a mechanism separating the locking bolt from the strike plate on the doorframe was heard as the door unlocked.

Connor pushed the door open and walked inside, taking off his heavy coat and hanging it on a hook attached to the wall. Devereaux followed and did the same.

The carpet was worn, but still in reasonable condition, yet it reflected the age of the house. Across from the entry and to the right, was a large living area furnished with sofas from the late 60's early 70's. It was like stepping back in time.

The green and orange fabric that covered the cushions on the sofas had seen better days. But what stories they could tell of Cold War goings-on! The secrets spoken by those who sat upon them and the lies that were perpetrated to meet an end's need.

Devereaux couldn't help but wonder if this mission was a lie too.

Connor sat on the retro sofa next to Devereaux and placed a manila folder on the coffee table in front of him.

The file was inked with serrated red stripes around the edge of the file. Large black lettering stamped the classification at the top and bottom of the file as "TOP SECRET". A smaller, yet equally visible, cautionary alert in red ink read "AUSTEO", indicating that the file was only for Australian Eyes and in this particular instance, it meant that very few sets of eyes were permitted to see inside and handle the file. Across the centre of the file was the name of the operation, "BRIMSTONE".

Inside, and fastened in the top left corner of the file, was a shoelace type fastener with a red fixing disc that was threaded through each page to prevent the paper from falling out.

Connor then passed Devereaux an envelope containing four photographs of Getti.

Getti looked fit, even if he did have a few extra pounds on him. He had a chiseled chin and strong facial features that beckoned respect.

His eyes were dark brown and piercing. He was not your average Thai soldier; instead, his image emanated his upper-class status. He stood out, a fact that had seen him move up the ranks and into elite social circles. The next two photos showed him with his wife and with his two children, one boy and one girl who looked to be in their early teens at the time of the photo – there was no date stamp to indicate when it was taken. The background of the picture was that of the Thai Royal Palace, which again demonstrated his access.

The fourth photo, taken by an unknown source, depicted Getti with Karen guerrillas up on the Thai-Burma border, not far from Mae Hong Son, 126km northwest from Chiang Mai in Thailand's north. Getti was standing next to a Pilatus Porter PC-6, a small taildragger type aircraft with a short take-off and landing capacity. The Porter in the photo looked grey and was complete with shark teeth painted on the front just below the engine.

The fuselage was adorned with the Thai military insignia.

Getti was standing in the foreground, talking to a man with his back to the camera and dressed in civilian attire. In the background were three men, two of whom looked to be Thai. They were loading the plane with a number of parcels around 30cm x 20cm x 10cm in dimension. One of the packets on the ground, waiting to be loaded, had a distinctive logo stamped on the outside – a Thai Naga. Around 30 to 40 packages remained on the ground. From the photo, Devereaux was unable to tell how many packets were already loaded.

The third person in the photograph caught Devereaux's attention. He looked to be European, possibly eastern bloc, he thought.

The man was huge in stature, with blond hair, a heavy-set square jaw, and muscular physique. In the photograph, he looked as though he was supervising the load. Devereaux looked at the date-time stamp on the photo, it was only a couple of weeks old.

Interesting! Thought Devereaux.

'Who is this guy, Connor?'

'I'm not sure, John – we're still working on that. Hopefully, we'll have the answer soon', Connor replied.

'Heroin?' Devereaux turned to Connor.

'Yeah, we predict 150 - 200kg or so' Connor replied. 'He's a busy chap, our General.'

Devereaux continued to skim through the file, stopping from time to time to take particular note of some detail – something that stood out, something that would give him an edge.

'What's this... Aran Gem Gallery?'

'We are not 100% sure, John, however, we believe the Aran Gem Gallery to be a shop in Aranyaprathet on the Thai-Cambodian border, and we believe it to be a front for his illegal gem business. He has been observed visiting multiple times – in fact, he goes there on the last Friday of every month like clockwork' Connor said.

'Is that so? Every last Friday of the month?' Devereaux asked in a sotto voce, his eyes glued to the file. His muttered question required no answer.

An hour had passed by slowly for Connor as Devereaux all but devoured the file's content. Standing up, Devereaux closed the file and placed it back on the table.

'I'm going to need a few things.' Devereaux said as he walked over to the window and looked outside, the sun pouring through the pane of glass. 'I take it I have open slather on equipment and any additional funds?'

'Just give me a list of what you need, and I'll arrange for it to be acquired in Bangkok', Connor replied.

'For starters, I will need both Safe Houses in Sukhumvit, and Hua Hin prepped immediately just in case they are needed.'

'They're both ready to go now' Connor replied.

'Great. I'll get the list of what else I need to you ASAP', Devereaux responded. 'In the meantime, I will need cash, mate – let's say $50,000 as an initial amount. I will need $10K today so I can get the ball rolling and get myself to Phuket at the earliest opportunity. That will be my entry point, and I'll pick up the remaining $40K for immediate expenses once at the safe house in Bangkok.

'I have $25,000 for you over in my office – you can sign for it on your way out' Connor said with a devilish grin.

'Will that be with a capital "X" Devereaux retorted.

Devereaux looked back outside the window, and was, for that moment, in deep thought. Turning back to Connor, he said,

'I have a contact in Thailand that can source all the toys I need, however; I will need some additional cash when I arrive in Phuket so that I am not carrying too much cash out of the country and causing undue attention at the airports. Let's say an additional US$200,000. That should about do it, I think. If I need anything else, I will let you know.'

'Oh, one last thing - passports?'

'They should be ready for you now or at the very latest by noon today.' Connor said as he stood and motioned towards the door.

CHAPTER 10

'Magnus'

DFAT, CANBERRA

09:40hrs

The early morning sun streamed through the window on the fifth floor of the Department of Foreign Affairs and Trade building in Canberra. Filtering through the blinds on the window, the pale amber colour cast lines of shadow and light across the dark blue carpet of Director General Magnus Webb's office.

Webb had just returned from briefing the Minister on affairs that occurred over the past 24 hours. He leaned back in his chair, his feet up on the table. He was angry!

Magnus had worked in ASIS for thirty years; most of that time as an IO and as a NOC. He rose through the ranks of the secretive organisation and had solidified an almost perfect reputation for his ability in getting things done.

A practitioner of the Cold War, Webb had learned that the world was not Black and White, but shades of grey. During the eighties and leading up to this moment in time – 1991, Perestroika, the political movement mostly attributed to Gorbachev to restructure the Communist party and move the Soviet Union into a period of Glasnost or Openness; made the world think that the Cold War had ended.

Magnus knew that the Cold War had never really concluded, but rather, it had merely stepped back deeper into the shadows. As an up and coming IO and possible Directorship of ASIS being considered down the track, Webb was quite apt at reading the signs, something the upper echelons in ASIS recognised and at times, bought him in to provide his thoughts and insight.

He was respected – he was going places within the Firm. In recent years, he had seen a change in Australia's political landscape, where politicians were becoming more complacent and more focused on political correctness and personal gain. They had become naïve to the realities of the world – a fact that Webb had grown increasingly resentful of. With the ever-present rotation of politicians through the seat of "Minister of Foreign Affairs and Trade" and by virtue of the position, they were his boss. Such

143

Ministers would come and go – they were civilians, untrained, unfocused and adolescent on matters of intelligence. They had become focused on their personal gains that such a position provided.

Webb and his predecessors had always found it challenging to get Ministers to act on the intelligence they had provided. The current Minister of DFAT was just that, a fence sitter, a naïve man who only sort to develop his own career through inaction – Minister Andrew McNeil was just that, a fence sitter in the guise of an astute politician. In Webb's eyes, McNeil was unworthy of the post.

He opened a manila file and rested it against his thighs. The file contained Top Secret material, which he used to brief the Minister. The information contained in the dossier was of the highest sensitivity. Inside the file and attached to the top document was a number of black and white photos. The photographs were of a scene of utter madness.

Bodies, torn and twisted, strewn about with their hands bound behind their back. Filthy rags were covering their eyes, and some with plastic bags over their heads that indicated a slow, agonising death.

The corpses were discarded into a shallow trench, more like purgatory than a place of rest. The remaining images showed the murderous assailants standing around their handy work. Amongst them, front and centre, was Abdurajak Janjalani, the founder of Abu Sayyaf... Madness... utter madness!

Yesterday, Webb had briefed the Minister for Foreign Affairs and Trade, Andrew McNeil, that after three years of searching they had finally located Janjalani and his upper echelon leadership group in the small coastal village of Luuk, situated on the far eastern end of Sulu Island in the southern Philippines.

Luuk was a known Abu Sayyaf training camp, but in the past, it had never been the location of a leadership gathering such as this. The photograph in Webb's file was taken from a gravesite located on Bitinan Island, 13km from Luuk.

According to the ASIS asset, Bitinan was an Abu Sayyaf killing field where they took those who did not comply with their doctrine to be executed.

The report showed several mass burial sites that resembled small mounds in the jungle in the central part of the island.

Given that Janjalani and his leadership team were all in one place, a rarity as the faction prided itself on disbursement, Webb advocated the use of an F111 strike on the meeting place to eradicate the terrorist leadership group and prevent – or at least retard – further terrorist attacks in the region. It was a once-in-a-lifetime opportunity, and Webb had explained the importance of what such a find meant to counter-terrorism efforts in the region.

McNeil was hardly moved, and his ambivalence was maddening at best.

McNeil was a fence sitter, a typical politician who enjoyed his paycheck and all the perks that came with such a seat, was happy to avoid making decisions when and wherever possible.

In Webb's eyes, McNeil was a coward and didn't deserve to be the Foreign Minister.

Webb hated working under McNeil, and yet that was the reality. He had to put up with his fence-sitting, his ignorance and his arrogance.

'Magnus, what you are asking is for a first strike incursion into a sovereign country, do you have any idea what you are asking of me?' asked McNeil.

'I know exactly what I am asking of you, Minister. I am asking for you to save the lives of many from future terrorist attacks.' Webb replied with some vigour.

'We can't just fly an F111 over the Philippines and drop a bomb and expect no recourse from the Philippines, let alone the UN.' McNeil responded as if to dismiss the idea outright.

'What I am asking of you Minister, is to make a call to your counterpart in the Philippines and discuss a joint operation to eradicate what is obviously a clear and present danger to our region's security. You are aware that Corazon Aquino is scheduled to have talks with Abu Sayyaf later next month, right? We all know she will concede Filipino land to this murderous Islamic movement as an autonomous region, giving them free rein to train as well as a place in which to carry out their murderous operations. Further, one would have to be a right moron to think that Abu Sayyaf will stop there, they will continue to spread until they have their caliphate.' Webb insisted.

'Ok, I hear you. I will make the call', McNeil said with some annoyance. Webb knew that McNeil would do nothing of the sort, rather, he would fence sit and avoid creating waves and indeed would make no such call.

This frustrated the hell out of Webb. At this morning's meeting, McNeil had said that any operation to hit Abu Sayyaf was out of the question as his Filipino counterpart had stated it would be counterproductive when talks between Aquino and Abu Sayyaf were so close.

The Philippines Government had long hoped for some form of peace with the Moro National Liberation Front

(MNLF), and now that most of the MNFL fighters had joined Abu Sayyaf, the Philippines Government was tired and didn't have the moral fibre to see any prolonged fight through.

Ahh... and there it was, the lie Webb knew would come.

'I know you are disappointed, Magnus,' said McNeil.

'Disappointed?' Webb looked at McNeil with steely eyes. 'Our team works tirelessly for years to find these monsters; putting their lives on the line, using valuable resources, not to mention taxpayer money, and for what?' asked Webb.

'When are we ever going to take the advantage when something is dished up to us on a silver platter rather than sitting back indolently and waiting until more innocent people are slaughtered?' asked Webb.

'I know Magnus. I understand your view and frustration; however, it's up to the Filipinos to decide what happens on their soil. We can't interfere if we are uninvited.' Said McNeil.

The fight against terrorism and all others that would seek to harm us, with the current diplomatic niceties, at least as far as Webb was concerned, was like pissing into the wind on a blustery day. Webb closed the file and threw it on to his desk, removed his glasses and closed his eyes, rubbing them with his thumb and index finger. When he next opened them, he was looking out the window. At that moment, he knew that the clandestine project he had been considering, and indeed working on – a plan that would turn the tables on terrorists and the underworld – was more needed now, than at any other time in Australian history. If Webb executed his plan, the enemy would no longer feel safe to run their enterprise of greed, violence and terror - Webb had decided that it was time to throw down the gauntlet.

Picking up the phone, he dialled a number.

'Hello,' said the voice on the other end of the line.

'Meet me in thirty minutes for coffee.' Said Webb.

The man on the other end hung up the phone without a word.

Webb partially lowered the receiver away from his ear and paused for a few seconds, thinking of his actions. Then, with a sense of justification, he hung the receiver back up. He knew that what he was about to do was against the law, but he also knew it had to be done because no one else would!

Webb grabbed his coat and walked downstairs and out on to Parkes Place, and walked along the footpath towards the High Court of Australia.

As he crossed King Edwards Terrace and onto the walkway leading up to the entrance of the High Court, he looked up at the great glass façade of the building.

The imposing structure was an ominous reminder that what Webb was about to embark on, was something so highly illegal, that at some stage, could see him staring at seven judges clad in their red robes behind the daunting judicial benches inside. It was almost like the building had eyes and was looking down on him with a questioning frown.

As he walked alongside the cascading ponds leading off of the Court, he turned left and walked through Nara Park and down under the International Flag display along Queen Elizabeth Terrace and across the road to Dom's Coffee Bar on the banks of Lake Burley Griffin. As he approached the café, he scanned the area for the man he was to meet. Breathing out slowly, Webb shook his head.

'Bastard', he muttered to himself.

Webb walked up to the counter and ordered two large coffees and then moved closer to the water's edge and sat on a wooden bench, waiting.

Glancing to his right, a long row of cherry blossom trees contoured the edge of the massive lake. Walking along the sidewalk under the cherry blossoms was a familiar man, his walk more like a fast shuffle, wearing an old Stratford tweed flat cap and with both hands in his coat pockets. It was Connor.

Webb sat on the wooden bench, sipping his coffee as Connor approached.

'You're late, you cheap bastard, arriving just on time to not have to buy the coffee.' Webb said as he started to laugh.

'And you fall for it every time, Magnus' Connor retorted and smiled broadly. 'Thanks, mate,' he said as he picked up the coffee and sat next to Webb.

'I've just come from briefing McNeil.' Webb said.

'Well, the fact that we're here so soon after that briefing isn't a good sign.' Connor interjected.

'Yes indeed, it didn't go well, but it was, however, unfortunately very predictable. McNeil is not willing to do anything proactive, rather he always has an excuse for not taking action. I am sick and tired of such inaction, placing our staff in harm's way, not to mention the safety of our assets.' Webb explained.

'As a result of the continued inaction, I have decided we are going to make a difference. I'm going to execute 'Mortimer Acquisitions.'

I spoke to you about this some time ago, and since that time, I have been forging ahead with establishing a facility for Mortimer Acquisitions in Sydney.' Webb added. Webb raised his coffee to his lips and sipped it.

Looking out over the lake, Connor turned towards Web, 'So, we are finally going to make a difference?' he asked.

'Yes ol'chap, we are going to meet terrorism and the underworld head-on with extreme violence, something that our foes have not experienced before and are not prepared for.

We will actively hunt them down, take or destroy their assets and terminate their very existence.'

'Why do you think I agreed to deploy Devereaux? I want to see firsthand how he handles this operation and what collateral fallout there will be.' He added.

Connor looked over at Webb and studied his face. Webb was undoubtedly angry and frustrated, but so was Connor – both men were tired of the bullshit that Politicians espouse, they were fake, plastic people who had no idea what was really going on. When they were given substantial evidence, they still could not fathom the real world around them. Instead, they retreated into a faux utopia, pretending all was in harmony.

'Devereaux will do just fine, he will not allow himself to fail' Connor said.

'That may be so, but I want you to be on a plane tonight for Bangkok and to provide whatever assistance you can. How do you feel about Devereaux coming on board and working Mortimer Acquisitions?' Webb asked.

'I was going to suggest that I recruit him into the service, and he works alongside me in the Deputy Director role.' Connor replied.

'No, not in the service – let's keep him solely as a NOC, as within that framework, he can be the most devastating. Let's see how Brimstone goes, and we can cross that bridge when we get to it, but I have to say, I am impressed so far. He will be a powerful asset, indeed.' Webb added.

'Walk with me.' Webb said.

The two got up and walked along the footpath under the cherry blossom trees. The cool breeze coming across the lake made Canberra cooler this time of the year than usual.

'What we are about to do Connor – and I really don't need to tell you this – is highly illegal.

As I wandered down from the office, I walked past the High Court, and it was as though the imposing building was talking to me – asking me if this is what I really want to do. The answer I told myself was a resounding YES! But I need to ask you, Connor, how do you feel about this?' Webb asked.

'Jesus Magnus, you really have to ask?' replied Connor. 'I have been waiting for over 20 years for someone with balls to take the role of Director General, now you're here, and Mortimer Acquisitions is coming to fruition. I'm in all the way.' Connor stated.

'I will head off to Bangkok tonight and monitor Brimstone from Pattaya and provide assistance from within obscurity.'

'You need to make sure there are no attributes.' Webb stated with some vigour.

'That goes without saying, Magnus.'

'If this goes well, and if Devereaux comes on board, we will make a real difference, but a difference that sheds no light as to the reason why these enemies are disappearing.' Webb said with some surety.

Webb stopped and turned towards the lake, looking over the water, then turned and shook hands with Connor.

'Stay safe old friend.' Said Webb as he turned and walked back towards his office. As he walked along Kings Avenue, he stopped at a payphone. Entering the phone booth and shutting the glass door behind him, he fossicked around his coat pocket for some change lifted the receiver and dialled a number.

The phone purred as it rang and then the call was answered by a woman.

'Hello.' Said the soft voice.

'Execute Mortimer Acquisitions.' Webb said.

'Acknowledged, execute Mortimer Acquisitions.' She replied and hung up the phone.

There was no turning back now. Webb replaced the phone and exited the phone booth. While he was walking back to his office, his mind considered all the consequences and all of the possibilities.

CHAPTER 11

'Anchalee'

BANGKOK

05:00hrs

The chirping of the alarm clock broke the uninterrupted slumber of Anchalee, and she peeled back her blankets and swung her feet out of bed. She squeezed the shag pile carpet between her toes and looked through the matted mess that was her hair.

She looked over at the alarm clock that flashing a red 5:00am. She sat upright for a few minutes, almost in a state of meditation, her back straight as a board, her eyes closed and her breathing deep and controlled.

She reached across and pressed the alarm "off" button, then eased herself up and stood, turning back to her bed and reaching under the pillow to retrieve her much-favoured 9mm Glock-19 pistol. As if on autopilot, she walked across the 33rd-floor apartment, pulled out a chair from her dining table and expertly stripped her weapon.

She walked to the kitchen, and from under the sink, retrieved a rolled-up valise and walked back to the table, unrolled the valise to reveal a weapon cleaning kit.

Every morning, without fail, Anchalee carried out the same routine, cleaning her pistol and checking all the working parts for serviceability.

She unloaded all the ammunition from the magazines to ease the tension on the magazine springs and cleaned each round before feeding the bullets back into the magazines. She left nothing to chance; making sure that her weapon came first, it was her highest priority of the day, her weapon of choice was her very survival.

She went to the bathroom and brushed her hair, and then pulling all of her hair to the rear, she gathered the remaining stands and pulled them into a ponytail.

Her long; silky, raven coloured hair reaching halfway down her back. She was a stunningly beautiful woman, even having just woken from her slumber, makeup-free, she was quite perfect, a fact that had made her life somewhat easier than most.

She wore black Nike waist to ankle running tights and a mauve Threadbourne Streaker tank top. Her mauve and black Nike Cross Trainer shoes looked like they had seen better days, no doubt from the countless kilometres of running. She placed a pouch around her waist and fastened the black plastic Delrin clip; picked up her Glock and inserted a twenty-round magazine; then cocked the weapon putting a round in the chamber.

Anchalee undid the zip and then placed the pistol inside the pouch alongside a silencer and refastened the zip. Anchalee made her way down the thirty-three floors to the foyer where she exited the building and immediately started running along the road for about 1km. Her run took her towards Bangkok's busy Silom Road that was beginning to get busy already, but not the usual deadlock that can be Bangkok. Looking left and right along the street, she found a taxi parked further along the road. The driver was lying back in the reclined driver's seat, taking a resting as Anchalee tapped on the window and asked if he was available. The driver, startled, sprang up with some gusto and bought his seat to the upright position.

'Yes, miss.' The driver sleepily replied.

She opened the door to the back seat and hopped into the taxi and said to the driver…

'Lumpini please.'

The 3km drive turned out to be rather quick, given the traffic at this time of the morning. Anchalee exited the taxi and started to run along the track that passed the Pagoda Clock tower in the southeast sector of the park. Her pace was slow at first as she warmed up her lean muscular body, her stride and cadence moving her effortlessly across the pavement.

She had covered 1km in 5 minutes; her body had loosened up, and her pace started to increase. The next kilometre completed in less than 4 minutes, the park was mostly empty, a few people here and there, but mostly the park and the running track was hers; all except two runners ahead of her, some 400 metres away.

One of the runners' cadence was hindered, more than likely due to the fact that he was carrying some weight; nevertheless, he was running anyway trying to lose some kilos. The man was in his mid-50's; his breathing heavy, his feet moving more like a shuffle than that of a running stride and his brow was heavy with sweat.

The other man, in his 30's was fit; he was wearing shorts and a lightweight tracksuit top that was unusual for running in this heat.

As Anchalee approached, she could see the second man had a bulge under his left arm that moved around as he ran…

'A bodyguard.' Anchalee thought.

She picked up her pace and closed the gap, trying to catch the slow runners, her breathing constant and unstrained. As the distance closed, she unzipped the pouch that was fastened around her waist, took out her Glock and attached the silencer. As she approached the runners ahead, she picked up the pace, scanned around the area for onlookers – it was clear. As she came up behind her prey, she raised her pistol and fired two shots in quick succession striking the bodyguard in the head.

The first round struck the C-1 cervical vertebrae at the base of the skull. The second round pierced the skull at the junction of the Parietal and Occipital bones, the bullets passing straight through, exiting the prey.

Before the bodyguard's body hit the ground, another two shots were fired into the back of the old man's head; both bullets entering the Occipital bone area of the skull.

Both runners collapsed instantly; their bodies lifeless before hitting the ground as if the Marionette strings had suddenly been cut. There had been no sound from the prey as they were slain, only the sound of the bodies as they hit the ground and the dull noise of the Glock's slide moving back and forth as an empty bullet casing was being ejected and another bullet being chambered. Both targets had their skulls torn apart; the contents spilled out on to the running track... they were dead!

Anchalee, not missing a beat in her cadence, continued past the two dead men, skirting the blood-stained pathway and continued her run as if nothing had happened. Unscrewing the silencer as she continued to run, she placed the Glock and the silencer back into the waist pouch, and secured the zip firmly. The assassin then looked down at her watch and started to accelerate her pace. Another ten minutes and she had completed the 5km run; her time: 19 minutes.

'Fuck, 19 minutes' she muttered to herself as she pushed the "stop" button on her watch.

She walked along the sidewalk and found a taxi and told the driver to take her to Sathon Nuea Road some 3.5kms from Lumpini Park.

After exiting the taxi, she started to run again, down towards the Chao Praya River, running along quiet laneways and narrow streets, periodically changing direction from where she had been dropped by the taxi until she was back at her apartment that was situated on the banks of the Chao Praya River.

The lifeless body of drug lord Zhang Ye and his bodyguard were laying on the running track in a pool of blood, several bystanders had started to gather around looking at the corpses. A woman was covering her mouth as she gasped in disbelief, while others just stood stared. Others just jogged on by, taking a cursory glance and continuing on - That was Bangkok!

As Anchalee entered the foyer of the apartment, the man at reception looked up...

'Good Morning miss Getti, how was your run today?' He asked.

'Good morning Danai, my run was great thank you.' She replied.

'Did you beat your best time?' He asked.

'No, not today Danai, my mind was elsewhere, I will try harder tomorrow.' She said as she pressed the button on the lift.

She entered her apartment and immediately went back to the dining table and stripped the Glock once again. She separated the barrel and put it to one side; then she pushed down on the slide plate cover and slid it off of the slide exposing the firing pin assembly. Turning the slide to the side, she depressed a lug and then removed the firing pin assembly and placed it next to the barrel.

She reached into the valise on the table and removed one of two sealed plastic bags and placed it on the table. She then commenced to clean her weapon thoroughly, then picked up the plastic bag and tore the bag open and removed a brand-new firing pin assembly and placed it back into the slide. She then opened the second plastic bag from the valise and removed a new barrel for her Glock and then reassembled the pistol, cocking it several times to ensure the working parts functioned correctly.

She placed the weapon in a leather holster on the table and wiped down the barrel she had used on the hit on Zhang Ye. She put the used barrel and firing pin assembly into the discarded plastic bags and wrapped them in clean tissue paper. She walked over to her bedside table and opened her black "Lady" Dior handbag and placed the barrel and firing pin assembly inside the bag.

The assassin walked into the bathroom and stepped inside the shower bay and started to take off all of her clothes, letting them fall to the floor. Picking them up, she placed them into a plastic bin bag and tied the top of the bag into a knot as she walked naked back through her apartment to the front door, leaving it there for disposal later on.

She walked back to the bathroom and entered the shower turning on the faucet and began washing her body well, paying particular attention to her hands and wrists for gunpowder residue.

She washed her hands several times, making sure every inch of her body was clean. She lathered her hair and washed it twice, using a large comb to secrete the shampoo thoroughly through her hair. After washing her body, Anchalee stood under the shower and let the water run over her perfectly shaped body.

Her eyes closed as her mind went through the checklist of her sterilisation drill, so she would leave nothing to chance.

Anchalee dressed in a dark grey Dior skirt suit; the tight-fitting skirt hemmed just above the knee, a sheer white blouse and black high heels shoes. Around her neck, she wore a single strand of pearls. She left her hair out to flow and cascade down her back. Picking up her handbag, and the plastic bag containing her running clothes and shoes, she left the apartment, and as she walked to the lift, she dropped the waste bag into the rubbish shoot; the bag plummeting the 33 floors to a dumpster below, which was cleared daily at 9am. By 10:30am, the bag and any evidence would be landfill.

As she walked out of the foyer, the man at reception asked...

'Shall I call for your car Miss Getti?'

'No, it's a beautiful day outside Danai, I think I will take a water taxi to work, have a great day' she replied.

'You to mam' said Danai.

Anchalee boarded a water taxi on the Chao Prior River, the private jetty for the water taxi was directly in front of her apartment building. The long skinny boat edged away from the pier and quickly built up speed.

After a minute or so at high speed, she opened her handbag and took out the plastic bag containing the barrel and firing pin assembly, then inconspicuously dropped it over the side of the boat where it sunk to the bottom of the murky, polluted Chao Praya River. After another five minutes, the long-tailed water taxi pulled up alongside a jetty, and Anchalee stood and disembarked the boat and walked up towards her office.

Looking out of her office over the river, she picked up the phone on her desk and dialled a number. A voice on the other end answered the phone.

'Yes – Designator please' said the voice.

'Alpha Tango Three, Six, Seven, Four' Anchalee responded, and then a paused.

'Wait; Alpha Tango Three, Six, Seven, Four'

'Secure' said the voice on the other end.

'Connect Three - Five – Seven' she directed.

'Connecting Three - Five-Seven.'

'Hello' said another voice, a man's voice.

'Go secure' Anchalee directed.

'Secure' said the man.

'Complete - Acknowledge' said Anchalee

'Acknowledge, Complete.' Came the man's voice.

Anchalee immediately hung up the phone without a further word. She made her way to the lift and went down to the lobby and walk across the road to Starbucks.

The early morning killing in Lumpini Park was just another day at the office for her. She killed with cold, callous indifference, as though she was a machine capable of putting any form of feelings to one side and then going about her day as if nothing happened. Such indifference made her an exceptionally dangerous and ruthless assassin. Her kill in Lumpini Park, Zhang Ye, a Chinese-Thai, was a rival to her father's empire.

He had a 30% share in the heroin trade, and Getti sought to take it from him. The assassination this morning was no doubt going to stir the hornet's nest, with all rivals now being on high alert. Yet, there was no evidence of who the killer was, yet the seed of distrust amongst the various NARCO families had now been sown.

CHAPTER 12

'Declan'

PHUKET, THAILAND

17:46hrs

The direct flight on Thai Airways from Melbourne to Phuket International Airport, flight TG-466, seemed to be over in no time. Devereaux slept seven hours of the nine-hour trip; his business class seat had proven to be a most comfortable ally. After passing through immigration and customs, he made his way to a taxi and proceeded directly to the Merlin Hotel at Patong Beach.

Devereaux was travelling light, with only a small backpack with two changes of clothes and shoes inside.

He figured he would buy whatever else he needed in the country, allowing him both flexibility in movement. It would also provide him with changes of clothing that he could use to make it more difficult for anyone that attempted to carry out surveillance on him.

He chose a room on the second floor overlooking the pool area. His room was small but comfortable. A large, queen-sized bed was the focal point, with high-quality linen and four soft pillows that lined the timber headboard.

Thai silk decorations adorned the walls, all depicting scenes from a time long since passed in Thai history. On closer inspection, Devereaux could see the intricate needlework on each piece, making the tapestry quite astounding. A small two-seat, rattan sofa was placed at the base of the window providing a beautiful relaxing view of the pool below, that was surrounded by palm trees – a small, well-hidden oasis.

After setting up his room, Devereaux changed into some board shorts and pulled out a white T-shirt with the Singha Beer logo on the chest - a fearsome lion from Thai mythology and a symbol of every cheap tourist in Thailand. He bent down to put on a pair of old running shoes that looked somewhat haggard, and he was done – dressed to blend into the rest of Phuket's chaos.

Devereaux picked up his near-empty backpack and walked towards his bedroom door. Taking one last look behind him to make sure everything was in place, he took the "Do Not Disturb" sign and hung it from the door handle on the outside. Before closing the door tight, he wedged a small piece of paper between the door and the doorframe in an inconspicuous location.

If the paper had been dislodged upon his return, he would know someone had been into his room.

Thawewong Road, the main beach thoroughfare along Patong Beach, was already bustling. Devereaux walked north along the footpath, its red paving bricks uneven and sparse in some areas, making it a trap for young players not on the ball. As he walked, he looked at the various small businesses seemingly all selling the same goods from store to store. Nevertheless, tourists were haggling away and buying, so the stores must have been doing ok.

The road was in good repair. The high curbing, designed for the tropical downpours, was painted in red and white stripes for ease of visibility in the wet, as well as for those tourists who were, perhaps, a little drunk and in need of visual aid to stay upright!

'Fuck, it's humid,' he thought to himself. Even at this time of night, the humidity was, and Devereaux was sweating viciously.

He stopped at a street store and bought a bottle of water that he devoured within seconds. Thawewong Road was bustling, with people out and about for entertainment. Restaurants were doing a brisk take, and the famous Patong bars were beginning to fill up with foreigners seeking their every pleasure.

Devereaux was continually updating himself with his environment. He stopped at a street vendor selling Polo shirts, knock-offs of course but excellent quality as Devereaux felt and inspected the material and stitching.

'Mister, how much you want' said the aging vendor, her teeth rotting from the beetle nut. Karen may be, Devereaux thought.

'Thao Rai Krup'? Devereaux asked how much for the two shirts in Thai. '20-dollar mister' said the vendor, the quick response challenging him. Devereaux looking around still surveilling his surrounds, then turned back and said...

'Paeng Maak' and smiled as he told the old woman it was too expensive and Devereaux started to walk away...

'Mai Dai. Mai Dai' shouted the old woman exclaiming it wasn't.

'Ok, ok.... 10-dollar mister' the vendor said.

'Dai' Devereaux replied, sealing the deal.

Devereaux reached into his pocket, pulled out $20 and gave it to the woman, and smiled as he walked away…. Knowing that even though he paid the original asking price, he won the haggle!

The old woman looked up at him and realised what he had been doing and smiled so hard, slapping the table as she bent over laughing as the funny foreigner walked away.

The redolence of food carts cooking on the streets and side alleys permeated the air. Food, spices and sauces being infused together under immense heat of the wok, offered passers-by a myriad of delicious tastes along with the persistent chatter of hundreds of voices. The sounds of two-stroke motorcycles and cars as they passed by added to the ambience, the intimidating sounds of their horns signifying to the unfocused to get out of the way. Such character dwelled in this place!

Above the streets were a myriad of black coloured power lines assembled in utter chaos.

They provided power to the brightly lit go-go bars and other business signs in the area, crisscrossing the roads and alleys and making the street seem like a cobweb filled with dazzling lights – something that beckoned the uninitiated to step into the parlour where nothing was, as it appeared.

On the ocean side of the road, the streets were lined with motorbike businesses for hire, their owners doing their best to make the tourists hire their death machines.

Devereaux leaned against the trunk of a coconut palm, looking down to his left. The mauve coloured roof of the Patong Police post stood quietly alongside the American icon Burger King, no doubt for those foreigners who couldn't quite see themselves eating something new and adventurous. The Police post had two well-dressed Police Officers, their uniforms immaculate and adorned with badges and ribbons with a revolver situated in a white holster that was worn snuggly on their hips.

Café de la Cruz: 22:36hrs

Café de la Cruz was situated diagonally across the road from the Police Post.

It was an old-looking Thai building that was most likely built in the 1970s. The timber shingles on the distinctive Thai-shaped roof had faded, with trusses and heavy timber beams holding it in place. There were no walls on the façade of the building, which allowed the cool breeze from the ocean across the road to filter through over the patrons. Inside the café were 15 tables - each seating four people, while another 10 tables and chairs were set up as alfresco on the outside of the café.

Music wafted outside gently to tempt passing foot traffic. At the moment, a Latin Salsa rhythm, Buena Vista Social Club's 'Candela,' was playing.

Café de la Cruz was a welcome oasis for many a foreigner from the hustle of Patong's nightlife. It was one of the only places where you could get a good coffee with fresh milk that was flown in bi-weekly from Australia. Tonight, the café was quite full and even from across the road, the scent of beautiful fresh coffee tantalised Devereaux's senses.

Devereaux could see a couple sitting on the inside of the café, close to the entry and fully engrossed in each other's' company as they held hands and were intent on melting into each other's' eyes. A man, European by looks, sat alone on the far right of the café watching the world pass by, his pint of beer clutched firmly in his hand. Other patrons filled the inside of the cafe – it was a typical night, just like any other. Outside in the Alfresco area, three out of the 10 tables were taken. A man in his late 60s, carrying far too much weight with white hair and a receding hairline that left vast swathes of his head open to the light and his skin was bright red from too much sun. He sat with a Thai maiden who was no more than twenty and dressed in ultra-short hot pants that left nothing to the imagination. His beer was almost finished - hers was barely touched, a common enough trick in Thailand to make foreigners by drinks to escalate their bar bill.

The left side of the alfresco was mostly vacant, bar one table, which had three working girls sitting at it. They were no doubt getting ready to go to battle in one of the bars; their time spent conning customers to buy drinks, gyrating on chrome poles affixed to the top of the bar and dreaming of a Knight in shining armour to taking them away to a better life.

Before approaching the café, Devereaux had been observing the site for almost an hour, moving from vantage point to vantage point and looking at the place from all angles.

Devereaux knew better than to walk into a place he didn't know how to escape from. He observed all the entry and exit points at the café, as well as the gaggles of people in and around it. He found every obstacle that could potentially prevent him from disappearing should something go pear-shaped. This was Tradecraft 101.

A group of 15 partygoers, filled with foreigners and Thai alike, moved along the sidewalk. Devereaux knew this was the time to make his move.

Manoeuvring himself to join the group as they moved up the street, Devereaux peeled off from the group as they passed the café and made his way to a table in the alfresco area. The partygoers continued along the street until their noise and antics could no longer be heard.

A waitress approached and gave the usual welcoming spiel, 'welcome to Café de la Cruz, sir, I'm Suchada, and I will be looking after you tonight. What can I get for you?'

She was maybe 20 years old with long, black hair worn in a ponytail hanging down to her waistline. She was slim and wore cut-off denim shorts and a black T-shirt ablaze with Café de la Cruz in white font across the front.

'I'll have a cappuccino please, and some Bruschetta' Devereaux replied.

'Where you from mister?' Suchada asked.

'I'm from Australia.'

'First time to Phuket?' she asked, curiosity evident in her bright eyes.

'No, I've been here a few times before', he said, hoping to quell further conversation before it drew unnecessary attention.

'Ok. Well, I won't be long, mister' and she walked to the counter to get his order started.

Devereaux was scanning the café and noticed a foreigner come from the kitchen area and talk to some staff. As the discussion concluded, staff members hurried away as if they had been given a new sense of urgency, no doubt by some encouraging words from the foreigner.

In his mid-30s with shoulder-length black hair and an athletic build, the man was fit. His arms were adorned in ink of a tribal nature while his muscle-riddled body indicated heavy gym sessions. Declan was a former team member in Devereaux's SAS team. He was Devereaux's forward scout and a highly proficient SAS Operative. After 10 years in the unit, he decided to discharge from the army and move to Thailand permanently.

Declan was on the fringe, always well-prepared and with a war bag second to none. Weapons, equipment, ammunition, and explosives – anything you needed to get the job done could be found inside. He was Devereaux's go-to man in Southeast Asia when he needed to be off the radar – but his services were not cheap!

Declan was standing behind the bar, facing a large mirror, as he prepared some drinks. He looked up and then back down, focusing on the task at hand. Then, as if to do a double-take, his eyes flashed up again and focused more deliberately at the lone figure sitting outside.

Devereaux!

'Fuck, what's he doing here?' he muttered to himself.

Declan looked at some of the order dockets and found the one for Devereaux's table, placing it in his pocket. Turning back to the bar poured two shots of Johnny Walker Blue into a tumbler and filled it with ice.

Suchada came to pick up the order, and Declan shooed her away, 'Forget this one, I've got it.' He picked up the tumblers and walked over to Devereaux.

'Your order sir', Declan said with a smile.

'Good to see you, Declan' Devereaux replied.

'Holy shit... I asked for a cappuccino and got top-shelf whiskey instead? Tell me, can you also turn water into wine' he added with a humorous grin.

'I'm surprised to see you.' Declan said.

'I was just travelling around and thought I'd call in to see how you are.'

'Bullshit, you would have messaged me in advance.' Declan retorted, looking at him with penetrating eyes, their intent obscured only by the smile visible for anyone watching the exchange.

'If anyone should ask why you spoke to me, Declan, say I'm an old army buddy on holiday and am staying in Phuket for the next week. Tell them I just came by to say 'hi'.' Devereaux returned a smile of his own to mask his words.

'You haven't changed, John – always on the fucking job. Are we going operational?' Declan muttered.

Devereaux looked up at Declan and said directly without answering his question.

'I'm staying at the Merlin Hotel up the road. Let's catch up tomorrow morning and discuss old times.' He said.

Declan broke his glance with Devereaux and looked across the road at an ominous black tempest sea and couldn't help but feel it was a sign of what was yet to come. He knew Devereaux well – well enough to know that darkness always followed Devereaux.

Whatever he was here for; Declan knew it wasn't going to be pleasant. Carnage and chaos always laid in his wake.

Declan looked back at Devereaux and said, 'sure, tomorrow at 0900hrs then. See you, poolside.'

And with that, Declan walked back inside and over to the bar to continue making drinks for other customers, glancing into the mirror to see Devereaux down the whiskey in one shot, place $20 on the table and disappear into the crowd in the street.

05:00hrs

The early morning was a welcome time of the day for Declan as he ran along Patong Beach. So little traffic, very little noise and the lack of people allowed Declan to clear his head and get some semblance of order out of the chaos that was Phuket.

He maintained a steady pace as he ran south along the beach. The tide was out, the sand firm beneath his feet as he pounded the beach towards Patong Bridge at the southern end of the bay.

As he took in the aqua coloured sea, he pondered the visitor that had turned up on his doorstep last night. Devereaux and Declan were friends and had relied on each other many times before in different hostile environments.

He trusted Devereaux and would do anything for him. He was surprised to see him though, but knew Devereaux, and knew he was on the job.

He would not come to see me unannounced, so he needs me to provide a service, he thought... a fact that made Declan change his demeanour into operational mode.

Declan continued his run back northward and gradually picked up the pace. The length of the beach was 2.6kms so by the end he would have run just over 5kms. The last kilometre Declan would do at top speed making his 5km run in just under 16 minutes.

The Merlin Hotel was terracotta in colour, with tiered floor levels draped with rich, tropical green foliage, that hung over each balcony giving it a feel that one would be in a hidden part of a far-off jungle. Its three pools were surrounded with multi-levelled palms of different types resembling an oasis.

Typical poolside bars were inactive at this time of the morning, but there was a hint of movement albeit subtle. The area around the three pools was littered with reclining deck chairs and next to them were large green umbrellas, which provided shade from the scorching sun that would soon beat down on Phuket.

Devereaux walked across to a group of deck chairs, removed a daypack and placing it between the chairs before taking a seat. A dense cluster of palm trees bordered the pool area and provided some privacy from the rear.

He had already ordered a coffee and some fruit and was now reading the newspaper, paying particular attention to the front page.

"Bangkok Times"

Friday, February 8, 1991

THAI SPECIAL FORCES

LINKED TO ILLEGAL GEM TRADE

BANGKOK, February 8: *Cambodia summoned the Thai Ambassador today, alleging the trafficking of precious gems orchestrated by high-level Thai military personnel.*

Cambodia alleges that over the past three years, a highly sophisticated operation to embezzle precious gems consisting of Rubies, Sapphires and Emeralds, has been underway and the Cambodian Chief Prosecutor, Mok Sen, going so far as accusing Thai Special Forces of masterminding the embezzlement.

According to Chief Prosecutor Sen, along with Reuter's journalist, Steven Quinn, said that General Sompon Getti, Commander of Thailand's Special Forces Division based in Lop Buri, was responsible for orchestrating the embezzlement.

It is estimated that since 1988 to the present day, more than US$18,000,000 of gems have been stolen via the sophisticated embezzlement operation.

Thailand's Prime Minister Anand denied such allegations and labelled them as absurd and most disappointing. Diplomatic efforts are continuing.

'Well, this complicates things", he said to himself quietly. Devereaux folded the newspaper and placed it on the table between two chairs. There was no doubt the new exposé would make Devereaux's task more difficult. Now that Getti was being scrutinised, he would have to look carefully at his strategy in order to complete the mission successfully. Devereaux never thought it was going to be easy – hell, such tasks were always harder than initially thought.

As Devereaux pondered his plans, Declan walked through the hotel and made his way to the pool. The hotel had the luxury of three of them, with the largest in the centre. That was the one closest to a large poolside bar. Devereaux looked up as he arrived.

'Morning mate.'

'John,' replied Declan.

'Coffee?' Devereaux asked, raising an eyebrow slightly.

'Yeah, I need a hit.'

Devereaux waved to the barman and asked for 'coffee' with a primitive hand gesture, pointing at the empty coffee cup next to him and holding up two fingers. Declan looked at Devereaux, smirked and shook his head, chuckling slightly.

'You learn those hand gestures at Harvard?' Declan mused.

'Fuck you – it worked didn't it?' Devereaux retorted with a smile and a laugh.

'So, how long are you here for John?'

'I'm not sure yet, but probably a month or so. Not here in Phuket of course', Devereaux replied.

'How are you doing for supplies, Declan?' he added, getting to the point of the visit.

Declan looked up at the approaching waiter as he delivered the coffee.

'Kawp Khun Maak Krup', Declan said, thanking the waiter in Thai and placing $10 on his tray before he returned to the bar.

'What do you need?' Declan continuing the conversation.

'There's a list of exactly what I need slipped between pages 8 and 9 of the Bangkok Times. Essentially, I need an AK-M with folding butt, six mags, 500 rounds of ammo, and an AK ammo vest – the canvas type, preferably aged with a lot of wear on it, but still serviceable. I'll need an RPG-7 with 2 x PG-7VL HEAT, along with a pistol with a silencer – 9mm preferably – and a quantity of ammo and mags', Devereaux said with a subdued voice.

'The rest will be on the list' he added.

'Oh, one other thing; I need a four-wheel drive, something reliable, that's prepped with some covert panelling for storing weapons, do you have access to a workshop?'

'The weapons are doable, but they are not here – they are over in Pattaya', Declan responded. 'As for a workshop, same – it's in Pattaya' he added.

'I need to go there next week anyway to check up on my other café' Declan said. 'Is that too late, Dev?'

'No, that's fine actually – time is on my side' Devereaux responded.

'That's a luxury, mate!' Declan said with surprise.

'I have a caché in my house on that side of the country. It's small, but it has what you need' he added.

'If I didn't know better, I'd say you're needing these too, let's say…. point the finger at someone else once the deed is done?' Declan asked rhetorically, understanding the question wouldn't be acknowledged.

'Is it secure?' Devereaux asked.

'What, the house? Yes, it's 100% secure – I built it myself, and no one even knows the caché is there.'

'Declan let me know the damage as soon as you can. In the meantime, there is a daypack in between our deck chairs. There is $50,000 inside it, which should get you started.' Devereaux said, his gaze fixed across the pool as he watched new guests being shown to their rooms.

'In addition to our cover story, if someone was to ask you about the cash I just gave you, it's a loan for renovating Café de la Cruz.'

'Got it' Declan replied.

'I'm going to get up and leave now, so stay here for another 15 minutes or so and then head out the same way you came in' Devereaux said.

He stood up and turned toward Declan, reaching out to shake his hand and saying, 'see you at the café in a day or two.' Then he walked away.

Declan did as he had agreed to do. He picked up the Bangkok Times and started skimming the paper. Just as Devereaux said, between pages, 8-9 was a small piece of paper, which he removed and placed in his right hand.

With the newspaper resting against his bent knees to provide some cover from view, he rolled the list uptight and slid the piece of paper between the lining of his wallet as he continued slowly turning the pages.

After 20 minutes, Declan reached down for the daypack, stood and hoisted it onto his back before folding the newspaper and leaving towards Thawewong Road, and walking back to Café de la Cruz.

CHAPTER 13

'Getti'

LOP BURI, THAILAND

Tuesday, 10:29hrs

'Yes, Sir.' The General said to the person on the other end of the phone.

'I can assure you, Minister, that the story is totally false, and I intend to take legal action against the reporter and indeed the newspaper and all those who have denigrated and impugned my good reputation. I...' The man on the other end cut in and continued his rant.

'Yes, Minister... Goodbye, Sir.'

Getti slammed the phone down, his voice was now devoid of any pleasantries. 'Get out!' he shouted, sending his aids scurrying for the door, as Getti glanced back down at the newspaper on his desk. The exposé from Reuter's journalist, Steven Quinn, naming him as the orchestrator of a large-scale embezzlement scheme boiled his blood.

'Motherfucker!' he seethed.

The phone call from the Minister of Defense had rattled Getti.

He sat in his office chair, the leather creaking as he swivelled from side to side, in deep thought. His hands rested on the edge of the wooden desk, his left ring finger tapping on the wood.

The gold military class ring was embossed with Thai script surrounding a blue sapphire that read, "Class of '67', the tapping sound echoing a rhythmic irritation.

A photo of his wife and two children sat in a gold frame on the right corner of his desk.

Directly behind him and high on the wall, as if looking down at him, was a portrait of Rama IX - King Bhumibol and Queen Sirikit.

The heavy ornate gold silk curtains were partially drawn, allowing shards of light to streak through and onto the floor, casting an image of the French windows on the red carpet.

Getti eventually sat forward, picked up the phone and dialled a series of numbers.

'Hello,' the voice on the other end of the line said.

'Meet me at the usual place in one hour', Getti ordered, and then hung up. He waited for the dial tone, then pressed five on the keypad.

'Yes, Sir?' the voice on the other end sounded like it just snapped to attention.

'Bring my car around now', Getti barked and hung up the phone with an arrogance his staff had become accustomed to.

The black 1988 Mercedes Benz 500 SEL pulled up outside the Special Warfare Command Headquarters at Camp Erawan in Lop Buri. The driver exited the car and raced around to the rear left-hand door to await his passenger. The dark olive-green uniform of the driver, three golden stars on his epaulettes, a young captain, was immaculate. Golden paratrooper wings on a red velvet background adorned the left chest of the driver.

A single row of ribbons neatly positioned below the paratrooper wings. The gold buttons running down the centre of his uniform jacket were highly polished, as was the shine on his leather shoes.

The brim of his peck hat was positioned perfectly and angled so that it was half-way down and central to his eyes.

The gold braided lanyard signifying he was the Generals Aid, not just his driver. The General's Aid stood, waiting patiently.

Getti exited the double glass doors to headquarters and briskly stepped down the stairs, his Aid saluting the General and quickly opening the door. Getti immediately entered the rear door of the car without returning the salute or even uttering a word.

The General made himself comfortable in the back seat of the Mercedes, but he was clearly irritable. The Aid, with a cautious tone, said:

'Good morning general, where would you like to go to?'

Getti looked up at the driver's rear vision mirror and made contact with his Aid.

'I'm sorry, Captain Kuchai, how rude of me. My mind is elsewhere this morning.'

'That's ok, Sir, where would you like to go?' Kuchai asked.

'Take me to the Lop Buri Inn on Narai Maharach Road' Getti said.

'I will only be there for an hour, so you can park in the car park and wait for me', he added.

'Yes, Sir' Kuchai responded, then pulled away from the curb.

The Lop Buri Inn was the newest hotel in town. Bragging six floors of luxury living, the Lop Buri Inn was undoubtedly a step up for the small town.

The façade of the hotel was painted white; however, the building had already started to discolour from the humidity and pollution from cars that passed by within a few metres of the structure. The building's design left a lot to be desired, its aesthetics were constantly at argument with good taste. Air-conditioning units adorned the front façade rather than being hidden away. Concrete planter boxes lined the narrow footpath just outside the hotel; filled with plants, some alive, some already lifeless. Pedestrians were having to turn sideways as they passed each other due to the space being taken up by the planters. Getti's Mercedes pulled up at the entrance to the hotel.

The Aid exited the car and moving briskly around to the rear left door where Getti waited for it to be opened – appearances were everything! The door opened, and Kuchai saluted the General as he alighted and walked into the lobby. The Aid, closing the door and moving back to the driver's seat, proceeded to move the car forward into a reserved VIP parking bay, where he would wait for the next hour.

Getti made his way through the lobby, turned right and entered the Panorn Wine Bar. A lone figure sat motionless at a table towards the rear of the bar, cigarette smoke suspended in the air in a haze around his table.

He wore a dark blue polo shirt and jeans, and some shabby Adidas running shoes. On the glass top of the rattan table was a set of keys with a faded keyring of an airborne unit.

Next to the keys, a pair of Ray-Ban 'Wayfarers' in tortoiseshell frames. The man was leaning back in the chair, his tight-fitting shirt proving he was an athlete of sorts and his dark, tanned skin an echo of his time outdoors.

The General approached the table and pulled out a chair, quickly sitting down and immediately reaching over to the pack of cigarettes on the table. The man raised his hand, flicking open a Zippo lighter and lighting the General's smoke.

'Thanks,' said the General.

Getti raised his hand to attract the attention of the waiter.

'Yes, sir, may I help you?' said the waiter.

'Two Chivas.'

'Yes, sir', and the waiter returned to the bar.

The two sat in silence until the waiter returned with their drinks.

The General raised his glass to toast the man, and they both drank the contents in one shot. Getti reached into his jacket and pulled out two envelopes, a manila envelope and a white envelope and passed both under the table to the man. The white envelope contained $10,000 while the manila envelope yielded a black and white photo and a single sheet of paper with biographical information of the target to be terminated.

'Find him and kill this Mother Fucker', the General said as he leaned forward intently. The man remained steadfast in position, his professional mettle without a kink – he was fearless.

'I want him dead by the end of the week – make it an accident. No, better still, I want his death to tarnish his reputation... I want this motherfucker totally discredited', he added.

The General, leaning back once again in his seat, raised his hand up to his mouth and took a deep drag on his cigarette, the smoke exhaled through his nose and mouth giving him the appearance of a dragon coming for the kill.

The man placed the envelopes down the front of his shirt, stood, put on his motorcycle helmet, and nodded at the General.

Without a word, he walked away.

Getti looked over at the waiter and held up his empty glass and signalled for another two.

The waiter delivered two more Chivas, and the General sat there in silence, pondering the hit he had just ordered. For Getti, this task could not come quickly enough – he had to get rid of Quinn, an impediment to his operation and a thorn in his side. Getti was very well-liked and adored in the upper echelons of Thai society, a position he needed to maintain if he was to wield influence in Thailand's strict vertical structure.

The Minister's call this morning was a reminder that everything he had built so far, could so easily come toppling down if he was not careful.

He would need to do some cleaning, a task that was well overdue. Since Pim's death, there were rumours that Getti was involved, but nothing that would stick of course. Nonetheless, rumours, stories and scandals create questions, they produce smoke where smoke shouldn't be.

Once Quinn was taken care of, and his reputation was back intact, he would start to create distance between his public self and his ruthless drug kingpin alter ego.

Getti was all too aware that his position in Thailand's social elite was only possible by his military prominence and reputation. Such a position opened the door to benefits unseen by ordinary people, and it was this very position, that made him one of the most powerful men in the Southeast Asian region.

CHAPTER 14

'Quinn'

BANGKOK, THAILAND

Friday, 21:46hrs

The intermittent rain kept the usual large crowds away from Patpong Road on this Friday night; nevertheless, it was still vibrant and the night markets, which lined the centre of Patpong Road, were still doing a bustling trade. Vendors with the greatest expertise constructed the yellow awnings, which were vacant during the day. Framing, lighting, yellow tarps, trestles and stock all needed to be set up and in sync with each vendor; all constructed within an hour and a half and ready for the tourist dollar. Steven Quinn left his office on the 36th floor at Reuters, located on busy Rama IV Road, opposite Lumpini Park in the Silom district of Bangkok. He exited the building and walked down the red-bricked stairs to the road, reaching up to undo a button on his maroon coloured shirt in response to the humidity. Sweat was generating rapidly after spending all day in his air-conditioned office.

He carried a dark brown leather satchel draped diagonally across his chest from the right shoulder. Inside the bag, a laptop, two 3.5" floppy discs and manila file containing all his notes that he was working on regarding a pending "Breaking Story" that promised to blow Sompon Getti's illicit operations right out of the water.

This was Quinn's big break as an investigative reporter – a story with such magnitude that he would finally make his mark as a serious journalist. Quinn had been waiting for this story all his working life and saw it as a means to solidify his position at Reuters in hopes of eventually securing his spot as a Bureau Chief. He had kept the details of the story close to his chest, only releasing enough information to entice interest so that he could run with it. His Editor, of course, was somewhat more eager to get the story out but knew what was to come would be one of the biggest stories the Bangkok Times had ever run. Come Monday, the story would hit the papers, and Getti's world would collapse around him.

Quinn stood on the verge hailing a Tuk-Tuk, the yellow and blue, three-wheel death machine had an ornate Naga carved in chrome on the frame of the number plate with the number "666" stamped on it – so apt for such a vehicle!

Quinn hopped in the vehicle and said, 'Patpong' thank you.

The driver, in his sixties, with an acne-scarred face, revved the engine of the hell hound and forced his way into the traffic as the rain changed from a drizzle to a torrential tropical downpour.

Fifty metres behind the Tuk-Tuk, a Kawasaki 500 stood with its engine idling, carrying a man dressed in black and a pillion rider wearing a clear plastic rain poncho. The pillion rider was a woman, with long blonde hair. The man in black quickly guided his bike behind the Tuk-Tuk as it merged with traffic.

After fifteen minutes of dodging and weaving, the Tuk-Tuk had arrived at Patpong, the rain still pouring down.

Quinn handed the man a handful of Thai Baht and exited the vehicle, placing his satchel bag on top of his head in a feeble attempt to remain dry in the tropical downpour. He ran quickly across the sidewalk and into Patpong Road's night markets, sliding under the yellow colour awning to, finally, escape the rain.

Bright lights and noise provided Patpong with its world-famous reputation, vendors hustled, the odour of sidewalk food carts as they cooked up their delicacies, permeated the area, Go-Go bars throbbed with loud music and touts beckoning passers-by to attend their establishments of illicit pleasures.

Quinn was heading to the Safari Bar, an old bar that had been in Patpong for many a year. Its yellow façade and Zebra stripes were distinctive amongst many other bars on Patpong.

A blue curtain covered the front entrance of the bar, two cheap plastic tables and outdoor type plastic chairs were placed either side of the entrance.

A Mama San sitting with eagle eyes as potential clients passed by. Two young women dressed in short, body-hugging dresses touted for business.

A red pedestal fan forced cool air across the entrance and onto the Mama San. On the left side of the entrance and hung on the Zebra skin deco, was a large colour print of Tulips. The eclectic nature of the façade did nothing to take away from the interior of the bar.

The Safari Bar was a long and narrow establishment. Its massive wooden bar top was highly polished showing an ornate grain in the wood. Behind the bar, and against the wall, were several rows of shelving that was very well stocked with spirits from all over the world. Below the shelves was a row of fridges that kept the assortment of foreign beers ice cold. Against the wall on the right side of the bar were several booths covered in blood-red velvet. Towards the back of the bar were several bar tables on single chrome poles where clients of the Safari could stand around chatting to the array of young, scantily clad women.

As Quinn enter the bar, a bargirl latched onto his arm and said 'Hi, Mister Quinn. Good to see you again.'

'Have you seen Peter or Allan tonight?' asked Quinn

'No Mister, I haven't seen them yet' she replied.

Quinn proceeded through to the bar, squeezing his way through the dense crowd. The DJ was pumping Bon Jovi's "Bad Medicine", and many of the predominantly overseas crowd were happily singing along.

Quinn rested against the bar, sliding a bar stool to the side and ordering a Singha beer. As he waited for his drink, he swivelled around and scanned the bar for the two colleagues he had arranged to meet.

No sign of them yet, and he turned around to face the bar once again.

He had been in the bar for an hour and was just polishing off his third Singha when Quinn felt a body press against his, a girl edging her way to the bar to order a drink. After bumping Quinn, she turned and said, 'oh, I'm sorry! It's so crowded tonight.'

'Did I spill your drink?' She asked.

'No, it's ok. No problem', Quinn smiled and stared at the woman.

She was Thai but spoke with almost perfect English with a slight American accent, no doubt from foreign schooling.

She had honey blonde hair that framed her flawless face with glowing skin. She was tall for a Thai woman, maybe 180cm, but was wearing high heels for appearance and had a slim but well-proportioned body. She wore an expensive black dress made of the finest silk, the hem halfway up her thigh.

A businesswoman? Quinn thought. She was no bar girl, that was for sure. Quinn couldn't help but notice that her dress had a plunging neckline, showing her perfectly shaped cleavage.

'Can I get you a drink?' the woman asked.

Quinn looked up at her in surprise, paused, then said, 'Singha, please. Thank you.'

The woman asked the barman for two Singha.

Quinn looked at the woman and said, 'a beer girl too, I see?"

The woman turned and laughed, 'yes, I have to say I do like beer – it's a bad habit I learned in college' she smiled.

'What are you doing here at the Safari?' Quinn asked.

The music was loud, so the woman placed her hand on Quinn's forearm and leaned closer to him, cleavage centimetres from his face and lips close to his ear, and she replied, 'I was supposed

to meet some friends here, but I'm an hour or so late thanks to the rain. I think I've missed them. How about you?'

Quinn could smell the perfume emanating from her cleavage, and his eyes were transfixed on the beauty before him.

'Same, I was supposed to meet friends here at 8pm, but it looks like I am too late. They must have moved on', Quinn answered.

'What are you doing in Bangkok?' She asked, still leaning in to hear his reply.

'I'm a journalist at Reuters here in Bangkok' he said,

'How about you, what do you do?' Quinn asked.

'I'm in shipping, my dad owns a shipping company, and I look after the US facility in Los Angeles,' she replied.

'I'm only home for two weeks then back to the U.S. I was hoping to catch up with friends before I go' she added.

The barman delivered the two Singha's, and the woman passed one to Quinn, holding out her beer and proclaiming 'cheers!' with a seductive smile.

'What's your name?' asked Quinn.

'I'm Noi…. and you?'

'Steven.'

'Nice to meet you, Steven' Noi replied, holding out her hand, perfectly manicured nails ablaze with deep red nail polish.

'So what are you going to do tonight now your friends are not here?' Steve asked.

She took a long drink of her beer and looked back at Quinn, replying, "well, I might have another beer and then head somewhere quieter – it's too noisy here. How about you? Want to join me?' she added with a smile.

'Sounds like a great idea', Quinn said as he finished off his beer.

Noi followed suit and drank the rest of her beer and slammed the empty bottle on the bar.

She looked over at Quinn, leaning forward again, her red lips whispering in his ear, 'do you like wine?'

'Yeah, I love wine' Quinn replied with a smile.

She tossed her blonde hair and smiled, 'come on then, let's get out of here – my hotel has a great wine bar in the lobby.

It's walking distance from here' she said.

Quinn smiled and said 'ok, sounds great – let's go!' He paid the bill, and Noi grabbed him by the hand, leading him out of the bar and onto Patpong Road.

'I'm staying at the Montien Hotel just down at the intersection.' she said.

The lobby bar at the Montien was rather quiet, a pianist's soft music floating through the air.

'That's much better' Noi said. 'I can hear you now, and I won't be getting looks of daggers from the bar girls' she said, and they both broke into laughter.

'Do you like red or white wine, Steven?' she asked.

'I love both, but hey, it's my buy' Quinn responded.

'Let's get a bottle' Noi said with a flirtatious smile.

'The Château-Grillet looks nice' she added.

205

Quinn smiled back at her, then headed to the barman and asked for a bottle of Château-Grillet and two glasses.

'Cheers again' Quinn said as he held up his glass to toast.

'It's so nice to meet you' Noi said, 'and so nice to be able to hear your voice.'

The wine was sublime as both chatted and sipped their drinks.

'Will you excuse me for a minute' Quinn said.

Noi nodded and smiled.

Quinn stood up and then said, 'Wow, that wine has a kick.'

Noi started laughing and replied, 'Yes, I'm feeling it too' and smiled widely.

Quinn walked across the lobby and followed the signs to the restrooms.

Noi, observing her surrounds, stealthily slid her hand into her bag and pulled out a small piece of folded paper, making sure she kept it obscured from view. She then reached over in a nonchalant manner, picked up the bottle of Château-Grillet and poured wine into each glass before replacing the bottle and obscuring the glass from others.

She leaned forward as if to study the label and, as she did, poured the contents of the paper into Quinn's glass. The white powder sank effortlessly to the bottom, dissolving on its way down. She rolled the white paper up tightly to make a stirring stick and quickly mixed the wine. She had picked Château-Grillet thanks to its rich flavour – a flavour that would mask any additive, like the blend of crushed up Rohypnol and heroin she had just infused into it. The mix of alcohol and blended drugs would take fifteen to twenty minutes to start taking effect.

Noi picked up the bottle of wine and topped off her glass as Quinn made his way back, raising the glass to her lips and taking a sip with a welcoming smile.

Noi took another sip of her wine and then asked, 'feel better now?' with a cheeky smile.

'Cheers!' she said as she took another sip of her wine, prompting Quinn to do the same.

'You have some catching up to do, Steven. I'm a glass ahead of you.'

Quinn reached forward and picked up his glass, draining it entirely, and said, 'we can't have that, now, can we?' Quinn smiled as Noi reached forward and topped up his glass again.

She stared at him and said, 'you know, I'm really glad my friends weren't at the bar tonight.'

207

Quinn looked over at her and replied, 'to be honest, I'm glad I didn't meet up with my colleagues, either,' and smiled back at her. Looking over at Quinn with an alluring gaze, Noi said, 'well then, why don't we take that bottle and head up to my suite? We can continue this conversation there.'

She stood, grabbing the neck of the wine bottle. Quinn placed $150 on the table and followed her as she moved towards the lift; her body was pressing against his, arms entwined.

The doors opened, and they entered the lift. As the doors slid shut, Quinn pulled her closer and kissed her red lips, something he had longed to do from the first time he saw her. She placed her arms around his neck and kissed him back passionately, her tongue exploring his mouth. She was an expert in seduction, and every inch of Quinn's being wanted her. The doors opened, and Noi wiped the lipstick off of Quinn's lip, smiled with a cheeky grin, and said, 'mmm, you kiss nice – if I had known that, I would have let you kiss me much earlier!' She said letting out a teasing laugh.

As they reached her suite, Noi turned and leaned against the door, kissing him again. Her hand moved behind her back, sliding the key card into the lock, and they kept kissing as they entered the room, the door shutting behind them.

'Oh my god, that wine is strong' she said, 'an aphrodisiac for sure!'

She held Quinn's hand and led him over to the bed and started kissing him passionately. She sat on the edge of the king-sized bed and begun undoing his belt and unzipped his pants allowing them to drop to the floor.

Quinn's hand finding its way inside her dress and cupping her ample breast and squeezing her nipple as she removed his underwear and started to caress his manhood as she looked up at him. The scent of her beautiful perfume stimulated Quinn's senses and raising his consciousness to ecstasy even more. His head rolled back, in pleasure as she pleasured him, her fabricated groans of ecstasy only served to indulge Quinn's euphoric state. His head moving forward and as he opened his eyes and looked down at her.

She told him to sit on the bed, and he did, his eyelids began to close. He shook his head to stay awake, but ultimately, he lost the battle, and his eyes began to close. Noi slaps his face, and he tried to lift his head, but to no avail. The chemicals rushed through his veins, working perfectly, just as planned.

Using her thumb, Noi pushed back Quinn's eyelid to gauge his level of consciousness. They had rolled up and to one side.

She slapped his face a few more times just to make sure, but there was no doubting the effect of the drug; he was out cold.

With that, Noi's demeanour instantly changed.

The assassin walked over to the closet in the room, taking out a small black backpack and opening it on the floor. She took out a rubber tourniquet and a small black leather container.

Sitting on the bed next to Quinn, Noi placed the tourniquet around Quinn's right arm. She then put her fingers on his neck, feeling for a pulse to ensure he was still alive. Opening the zipper on the black leather container, she withdrew two syringes, both containing 5ml of heroin – 98% pure heroin.

The assassin lifted Quinn's forearm, tapped the skin to find a vein and then slid the needle into the pulsing vein. She pulled back on the syringe plunger to see if blood was being drawn back into the syringe and confirming she was in the vein. She released the tourniquet and then slowly injected the contents of the syringe into his arm. She then removed the needle from his arm, wiped it with a cloth removing her fingerprints and then rolled the syringe

210

across his fingers to plant Quinn's prints on the Syringe; then, placed it on the floor next to the bed.

The assassin, with a clinical demeanour, paused and watched Quinn's chest as it started to expand more slowly. She efficiently removed his clothes and propped him more upright against the headboard. He was completely naked and void of any senses. Reaching over for the second syringe, she removed it from the black container and again injected the contents into the same arm, this time leaving the syringe dangling from the forearm.

She sat on the bed and waited for the heroin to take full effect. Quinn's breathing started to become more shallow, then, with one long final breath, his body exhaled the remaining air in his lungs, and he was finally gone.

The assassin opened up his eyelid in a methodical fashion and looked into his pupils. They were fully dilated and fixed, only an empty soul peering back at her.

The assassin walked over to the TV stand and stood there looking back at her kill as well as the room around her, eyes scanning left and right.

She opened the backpack, placed on some rubber gloves and took out a cloth impregnated with an alcohol-based solution.

She cleaned his mouth and then, after it was clean, dipped her finger into some wine from the bottle and rubbed it on his lips. She wiped the dangling syringe in his arm clean, then placed the syringe back against Quinn's fingers, again transferring his fingerprints to the syringe, then propped his left arm across his lap. She took both wine glasses into the bathroom and washed them thoroughly, wiping them clean and placing one back in the cabinet. The other, she poured a small amount of wine into it and swished the wine around the inside, then put the glass against Quinn's lips before returning it back down on the bedside table.

The assassin then went about meticulously cleaned every part of the suite, wiping down every surface that she had touched.

She made sure the body was in the right position; she took out a plastic bag from the backpack and emptied the contents onto the bed next to the body, a selection of photos, child porn photos. She put them in place, close to the body and moved his left hand onto his genitalia, giving the impression he was getting sexual gratification from the photos at the time of his "accidental death".

The assassin did one last check of the room. Quinn's brown satchel was on the floor near the entrance. She picked it up, brought it back to the bed and emptied it. Foraging through its contents, she picked up a laptop, a manila file and some floppy discs and placed them into her backpack. She carefully placed the satchel next to Quinn's lifeless body, slid a couple of incriminating photos partially in and out of the satchel, and left the rest strewn on the bed next to the corpse.

Making sure everything was in place, the assassin left the room, pulling the door closed behind her and placing the "Do Not Disturb" sign on the door handle.

Passing through the quiet lobby and out onto the street, she weaved her way through the still bustling Patpong Road, turned left and entered a laneway, which provided access through to a parallel road - Patpong 2.

Part way through the alley, she stopped in the shadows, where she quickly removed the blonde wig and let her natural black hair cascade down to her shoulders and place a grey baseball cap on her head.

Bagging the wig, and other items from the hotel, she threw the items into a dumpster as the rain started to get heavier.

She dashed through to Patpong 2 and then turned right at the Club King Go-Go bar and proceeded as planned to Silom Road, keeping her head down so that her face was not easily recognisable.

She turned left and moved along Silom Road for about 100m where the man on a black Kawasaki 500cc motorcycle was waiting. Looking in his rear vision mirror, he could see his accomplice making her way towards him. He pressed the ignition button on the handlebars and revved the motorcycle engine. Passing a helmet to the assassin, she got on the back of the Kawasaki and secured the helmet.

'Is it done, Anchalee?' he asked.

'Yes, of course it's done, Chatri' she replied and then tapped him on the shoulder. He eased on the throttle and merged into Bangkok's notorious traffic and disappeared into the night.

CHAPTER 15

'Pattaya'

PATTAYA, THAILAND

Tuesday, 10:15hrs

Connor sat on a wrought-iron chair, his coffee on the small table next to him. The balcony, where he sat, overlooked Pattaya and its umbrella-covered beaches below. He had checked into his room on the 20th floor of the Holiday Inn Pattaya Hotel just the day before.

As he sat there enjoying the morning sun, he read page two of the Bangkok Times.

"Bangkok Times"

215

Tuesday, February 12, 1991

JOURNALIST DEAD

BANGKOK, (AP). A journalist was found dead yesterday in a hotel room at the Montien Hotel located in the Silom district. Steven Quinn, an American journalist, working for Reuters, was found dead of an apparent drug overdose. According to police sources at the scene, Quinn was found on his bed with a syringe still in his arm. A source said that Quinn was also viewing child pornography at the time of his death. Quinn's body was taken to the Bangkok Coroner's Office for further examination.

Connor saw more than the ink on the page. His experience as an IO had taught him that this story added more complexity to an already complex task. The death of a man ready to expose someone of great prominence, just 48 hours before the exposé, would undoubtedly raise eyebrows. It reeked of Getti, Connor thought. Of course, Getti would deny any involvement and have a perfect alibi distancing him from any wrongdoing. No doubt he will claim the incident was regrettable, especially for someone in the prime of his life, drugs had taken him far too soon.

Connor imagined that Getti would further distance himself by saying no more, leaving his press handlers to make any additional comments; such comments focusing on Quinn's drug use and his deplorable paedophilia. The operation to destroy Quinn's reputation had begun in earnest. At least that's how Connor saw it.

Connor put the newspaper down, picked up his coffee and looked out over the emerald coloured sea, his mind strategising on the way forward. This untimely but brief indisposition will need careful and thorough consideration. Postponing the mission was not an option, though Connor. UNTAC was looming, and any impediment to that mission would be intolerable as far as Canberra was concerned.

The other issue becoming ever more pressing was the volume of heroin coming into Australia. It had become more apparent that the heroin was coming in from Thailand. While they had no direct proof, it was agreed, amongst DFAT and the Australian Federal Police NARCO division that the most likely source of the heroin was a supplier that Getti had a distant hand on.

Taking another sip of his coffee, he pondered that removing Getti sooner rather than later would not only pave the way for UNTAC but would then, at least in the short to mid-term, cut off the volume of heroin supply from that particular source.

In doing so, there would be a knock-on effect. The power that Getti wielded, orchestrating military elements on the ground, the bribes being paid to police echelons along the way, and the pricing deals solidified, all of which was done to ensure the supply of heroin would go unhindered. If Getti were out of the picture, all of those deals would be null and void. A new power struggle would emerge, new deals would need to be made, and more money would have to grease the palms of delinquent officials.

It would be chaos and would take time for them to restructure.

It was 11:50 and Connor heard a knock on his door. Peering through the peephole, he saw Devereaux. Connor unlocked the door.

'Morning John, come in.'

Devereaux extended his hand as he walked in. Connor took it, and they shook hands as Devereaux walked past.

'G-day' Devereaux responded as beads of sweat dripped from his brow.

'A bit warm, mate?' Connor asked.

'Yeah, it's a bit warm out there.'

'Grab a cold one from the fridge, John. Did you happen to read the Post this morning?' asked Connor.

'No, not yet – why?'

'Page two – over there on the balcony table.'

Devereaux dropped his backpack on a chair and walked over to the balcony, picking up the paper and walking back inside. He sat on the sofa and opened the Post to page two.

'Well, that was quick' muttered Devereaux.

'I'll say – bloody quickly! We need to move a little faster on this. Getti will be in a state of high alert, making your role just a little more difficult' Conner added.

Devereaux looked over at Connor, his eyes amused.

'You think so?' he said.

'Well, if it were going to be easy, we would have got someone else to do the job' Connor quickly responded.

Connor sat on the sofa and told Devereaux to sit next to him. He opened up his laptop and turned it on. The screen lit up, and after a few seconds, the screen welcoming the user to the session. The last "used" notification splashed onto the screen.

"YOUR LAST LOGIN WAS: MONDAY, 11 FEB 1991 at 23:51HRS."

Connor took out a white envelope from his laptop bag. He opened it and removed a small 3.5" computer disk, its blue plastic housing revealing nothing – no labels, no markings; it was clean.

Connor inserted the blue disk into the computer. The computer read the disc, and an icon appeared on the screen. Connor opened the file and revealed several subfiles.

Connor looked at Devereaux and asked, 'remember when we were looking at the dossier on Getti at the Annex, and you had a number of questions?'

'We have some additional information, not much more since we last spoke, but we do have a better understanding of how Getti is operating' Connor added. 'Do you remember the photograph of Getti in Mae Hong Son, where they were loading narcotics into the Porter?'

'Yes, what of it? Did you find out who the European man in the photograph is?' he asked.

'Yes, we did. His name is Aleksandr Drozdov, and he is a former KGB officer – but now he's the Avtoritet in the Russian Bratva' Connor said.

'The Russian Mob... Bratva?' Devereaux asked.

'Yes mate, the Rossiyskaya Mafiya, "Vory V Zakone" to be more precise. His position, as we know it, is a

"Brigadier", that's like a Caporegime or Captain in the Italian mafia crime family in the U.S.

As far as we know, he reports directly to the Krestniy Otets, that's the Godfather back in Moscow' Connor said.

'We understand he is currently operating somewhere on the French Riviera, we are not exactly sure, but we are working on that' he added. 'The NARCO team believes Getti is one of their primary sources of heroin into southern Europe. Once I have more information on Drozdov, I will let you know.'

'The boys at the office have also been working hard on the photograph of Getti and his family, particularly his two children. MI6 were helpful and provided us with some interesting information' he continued. 'Chatri, Getti's son, and his daughter, Anchalee, are both Intelligence Officers for Thailand's National Intelligence Agency – the N.I.A'. Conner added.

'Now, that's interesting' Devereaux said. 'How the hell did we miss that?'

'There had been no real focus on the children up until now. We did know that both children went to the Thai Military Academy and were both stationed at Command, in Bangkok. After that, we concentrated in areas of higher importance – manpower issues, you see' Connor replied.

'I get it. Well, this certainly changes things. At least we know what we are up against.' Devereaux replied. 'What does MI6 know about them now? What section of N.I.A do they serve in?' he asked.

'We know via our friends at MI6 that they are both in Div-9' Conner replied.

'Div-9, that's International Operations. Do we know where they are assigned?' Devereaux asked.

'No, that's it at this stage, no other information just yet. I have asked MI6 for some follow-up information though. Let's see what they come up with' Connor added. He opened another file on the laptop. Photos of the Aran Gem Gallery appeared.

'We, unfortunately, don't have much new knowledge on the Gallery. We did have some assets surveilling the place, but there was nothing much happening there. We did see a particular customer returning several times – at least, we think it's a customer.

It was a woman, Thai by the looks. With limited information available, we really didn't get much. The photos didn't give us any facial shots, at least not enough to get positive recognition' Connor said. 'She did spend considerable time in there though, more than the average customer. We thought she might be a wholesaler.'

Devereaux looked over each file carefully, committing the images and information to memory.

'I think I will head out to Aranyaprethet' Devereaux said. 'Knowing that Getti visits the gallery at the end of each month, it could be our best opportunity. If we are going to take him down, that's where I will do it.

It's close to the border, and he now has enemies on the Cambodia side, and they hold him responsible for Pim's murder. If I can make it look like the Khmer made a revenge killing, then that's what we need' he added.

'I think you're right, John. That very well might be our best bet. Head out there at your earliest opportunity and get the lay of the land' Connor said.

'Did you bring something for me?' Devereaux asked.

'There is US$100K in the case, transfer it to your pack – and yes – sign for it!' Connor smiled, but his direction was clearly an order.

'Have you finished with this, John?' Connor asked as he looked at the laptop.

'Yes, I am done, thanks, ' Devereaux replied.

Connor ejected the floppy disk from the drive, and, using a small Swiss army knife, pried open the plastic housing and removed the magnetic disk. Leaning over an ashtray on the table, Connor used a lighter and began burning it. The disk melted into a tiny crumpled ball and after it had cooled down, Connor wrapped it in toilet paper and flushed it down the toilet.

The plastic housing, he gave to Devereaux and said, 'there, earn your money and dump this somewhere on your way out.'

Devereaux wiped the plastic housing clean of any fingerprints and put it into a small plastic bag, then shoved it into his trouser pocket.

'I'll be in touch' Devereaux said, and he reached out and shook Connor's hand.

'Stay safe, pilgrim' Connor said.

Devereaux rode his white and black Yamaha XT-250 trail bike north along Pattaya-Na Kluea Road. The telegraph poles, which lined the righthand side of the street, were strewn with hundreds of power and communication lines. Like that in Phuket, there seemed to be no rhyme or reason to the chaotic layout of the cables. It was a Thai thing, from chaos came harmony - The lines where the chaos, the electricity delivered to the household, the harmony. For some reason, it all worked out for the Thai's.

The road was a well-constructed, a dual carriageway and the traffic moved smoothly. Shops lining each side of the road and a myriad of "7-Eleven" stores were a regular feature.

Looking in his rear vision mirrors, Devereaux was frequently scanning his surrounds for any sign of a surveillance effort – looking for cars that were parked on the side of the road and might follow him from a distance and looking for anyone that might be paying more attention to him than out of the ordinary. He frequently changed direction, and sometimes turned around completely and came back the way he had come. If anyone were following him, he would know.

Turning right into Naklua-17, he followed the road for eight hundred metres and then turned left onto Naklua-19, following it for another two hundred and fifty metres before stopping outside a compound.

The two-metre-high electronic gate was made of steel and brown coloured timber – an ominous barrier at the entrance to the property. Either side of the gate was two square concrete columns clad with variegated coloured sandstone. At the top of the columns were cast-iron lamps, the same type of lamps were placed every two metres along the perimeter wall that surrounded the entire property.

Devereaux placed the bike stand down and walked over to the gate's intercom, pressing the button. A camera panned down, and a voice rang out, 'what the fuck do you want? And did you bring any beer?'

'Something better' Devereaux replied.

The gates began to open, sliding to the left and Devereaux maneuvered his bike through the gates and rode it up to the villa, parking under a large mango tree that was the central focal piece and pride of the garden.

Declan came out of the villa to greet Devereaux, dressed as casual as an Aussie could be - shorts, thongs and T-shirt were the order of the day. The house was a large single-story home with a terracotta coloured tiled roof. The exterior of the house was painted in a soft yellow colour, with trimmings around the windows a pale blue with a worn texture to the woodwork. The home had a South American feel to it, more like a hacienda than a Thai home. With all the large trees on the inside of the compound along the two-meter-high walls, the style of the house fitted in nicely, providing a pleasant sanctuary from the hustle and bustle of Thai life.

Devereaux walked over to the sofa in the living room, placing his backpack near the edge of the sofa and walking over to the large concertina windows stretched floor-to-ceiling. They were open to let what little breeze there was come into the house. Large ceiling fans turned as if they were rotors from a helicopter, a soft swooshing sound as the blades forced cool air down below.

The back garden had a swimming pool surrounded by limestone pavers; a few deck chairs alongside tables with a large umbrella fitted to the centre of the table to help ward off the sun. At the back of the compound, a smaller building, a guesthouse that faced back to the pool, yet offered privacy from the rest of the house.

In the living room, a row of monitors was active. The house was well protected; CCTV cameras covered each external property wall, providing coverage of the entire front and back yards as well as the sides of the property.

'Where are those images coming from that cover the areas around the outside of the house?' Devereaux asked.

Declan had the fridge door open and was grabbing Coronas when he turned to answer, 'I modified the lighting system on top of the wall. I placed a camera inside four of them so I can watch the perimeter and approaches to the property.'

'Nice mate, great coverage' Devereaux replied.

'Here Dev, get this into you' Declan said as he handed a beer to Devereaux.

'Ahhh, thanks mate, just what the doctor ordered. Cheers!' Devereaux said as he raised his beer.

Declan didn't say a word, just raised his beer and took a large swig before peeling his mouth away from the bottle and letting out a small sound of delight, 'Shit I needed that, it's bloody hot today.'

'Grab your pack and follow me' Declan said.

The pair walked out past the pool and into the cabana at the rear of the property. Inside and to the left was a bar and to the right were a number of sofas all positioned out towards the pool. Declan walked behind the bar and over to a small refrigerator; opened the glass door and pressed a button that was concealed next to the temperature gauge setting dial.

A gentle hummed permeated the air as an electric motor wound up, the floor behind the bar slid open and across to the right and under the bar. The opening led to a set of metal grated stairs that went down to a concealed room.

Declan reached to the right and turned on a light at the bottom of the stairs. He pinned in a code on the heavy iron door, and the door opened and a set of fluorescent lights arced into life.

'Welcome to my lair' said Declan.

Devereaux walked inside the room. Arc mesh-lined the walls of the twenty-foot sea container and hanging on the arc mesh walls were various weapons: M16's, M203's, AK-47's, AK-M's, RPD's, RPG's and a range of pistols and revolvers that laid alongside a range of knives and other unpleasant toys.

At the end of the room was a workbench, above the workbench, high on the wall was a replication of the CCTV monitors that were in the house.

Sitting on top of the bench was an M60 machine gun – new like it had just been taken out of the grease wrapping. It was partially stripped, a work in progress, perhaps, Devereaux thought.

Under the bench was an array of munitions, thousands of rounds of ammo, RPG Rockets, and hand grenades and some claymore mines. On the right side of the room, packed along the wall, were waist high weapons boxes stamped with 'M-60 Machine Gun. LOT 23791-4 2 EACH', while another box was labelled 'RPG-7 4 EACH.'

This was a soldier's paradise.

Devereaux looked over at Declan, who was standing at the door motionless. 'Fuck me... now I know where all my money goes' Devereaux said.

Declan laughed and said, 'Well, after today I can add to my collection', and he raised his beer and said, 'thanks for that, by the way'.

'Do you have what I ordered?' Devereaux said.

'Yes, it's all here.'

'The RPD Machine Gun, where is it from?' Devereaux asked.

'It's CHICOM, they were acquired in Vietnam' he said. 'Do you want the RPD?'

'No, I will take an AK-M's and one RPG and associated ammo as discussed. However, this H&K USP pistol, I'll take right now, do you have three mags and a silencer?' Devereaux asked.

'No problem' Declan replied, reaching into a drawer and pulling out the silencer and three mags and handing them to Devereaux.

Turning and walking back towards the door, he bent down, opened an ammo box and pulled out a box of 9mm Parabellum.

'Will 100 do?'

'Plenty', Devereaux replied as he continued checking out the condition of the pistol, quickly stripping it down and inspecting each part for wear and flaws, then reassembling it as if it was second nature.

'So that's it, then?' Declan said with a disappointed tone.

'Yep, but don't worry, I will pay you for the original order' Devereaux said with a smile. 'All of the serial numbers are ground off?' he asked.

'Yes, everything here is untraceable.'

'Did you get the car I wanted and have the modifications made?'

'Yes, it's parked at the front of the house' Declan replied.

'The white Toyota Land Cruiser?' Devereaux asked.

'Yes, all done' he replied.

'Full tank of gas?' Devereaux asked with a smart-arse smile.

'Fuck no, that's extra' Declan retorted, and both started laughing.

Back in the house, Devereaux sat on the sofa and pulled his backpack closer, placing it on the floor between his legs. Pulling back on the drawstring, he opened it up.

'So what's the damage?' Devereaux asked.

'All up, US$60,000, and that includes the vehicle' Declan replied.

'Here's US$80,000. That's $20,000 I have in credit with you just in case I need something else.'

Declan nodded.

'Ok, give me a receipt for the cash' Devereaux said.

'Sure, right after you give me a receipt for the weapons' Declan quickly retorted, and both smiled.

'Dec, I need the car to be positioned at the Inn Pound Hotel in Aranyaprethet on Monday the 18th. I know you don't have much time, but my schedule has moved up. Can you load it up with my gear and have it delivered there no later than 1700hrs on Monday?'

'The driver can park the vehicle in the car park. He needs to ensure it's locked and get him to return to Pattaya by bus.

Take the expenses out of the $20,000 and make sure he is well paid. He can leave the key to the car on top of the rear diff' he added.

'No problem, I have a guy perfect for the job' Declan replied.

CHAPTER 16

'ARAN'

ARANYAPRETHET, THAILAND

Monday. 15:49hrs

The stretch limo turned right into Chaoprayabordin Road, at least Aranyaprethet's version of a stretch limo. The Tuk-Tuk was very different to those in Bangkok. At almost twice the length of a normal Tuk-Tuk, this hardy, ornate vehicle had seen better days, yet it had room to seat five passengers and ran flawlessly. Built on a stretch chassis, the Tuk-Tuk boasted a 750cc Honda engine that was encased in a mesh-like a chrome steel cage. The handlebars were more like something from Peter Fonda's chopper in Easy Rider, and the driver of the Tuk-Tuk was proud of his hell on wheels.

'Yud thī nī thāng ŝāy' Devereaux said, telling Easy Rider to stop here on the left.

The driver pulled over at the corner of Chaoprayabordin Road and Bariwendan Road, just outside Kim Kim's Café.

Devereaux paid the driver, placed his backpack over his shoulder and walked towards the entrance doors to the café.

He stopped as if to look at the menu in the window and used the reflection in the glass to observe around him.

People were going about their daily business, the odd delivery van stopping here and there, their vehicles doubled as the drivers raced inside to drop their delivery. The noise of scooters and small motorcycles pierced the air as they scurried by.

Kim Kim's was a favourite meeting place of Aranyaprethet's upper-middle-class, and one of the only places in Aranyaprethet where you could buy a half-decent coffee.

The façade was unusual. Its roof was made of sheet tin that extended out over the sidewalk and ran flush with the curb below, allowing the heavy rain to wash from the roof and straight out onto the road. More intriguing, however, was that the roof was built around a power pole secured into the street below. The pole itself passed through the ceiling and through the roof, with an electricity cable stretched only half a meter above. Such adaptation always amazed and perplexed Devereaux.

Pulling back on the curved chrome door handles, Devereaux entered the café and chose a table away from the windows while still offering him a good view of the streets outside.

The café had eight tables inside and a large glass refrigerated cabinet filled with French pastries. The selection was quite impressive, Devereaux thought as he perused the delights on offer. He ordered an Americano coffee and Apricot Danish that looked far too good to pass up.

Sitting back down at the table, he maintained a watch on the comings and goings of the people outside, paying particular attention to that of the authorities; how often they used this road? How many of them would pass by at any one time? What type of vehicles did they use? How fast were they driving? All these questions raced through his head. This road is of significant importance to Devereaux as the Aranyaprethet Police headquarters was only 1.5 kilometres away. Of course, he knew he would not know their best response time unless there was an actual emergency, and he could assess their capability.

A supposition would have to be made based on Devereaux's extensive knowledge of Thailand, its support apparatus in terms of emergency services, military and the police, their level of training, Aranyaprethet's geographic location, and the districts municipal financial budget. All of these things would help determine response times.

Devereaux had spent the last couple of hours observing the street, and it was now 18:30hrs. He stood to leave the café, flicked his backpack over his shoulders, placed 400Baht on the table and stepped out onto the street. Walking south along Chaoprayabordin Road, Devereaux observed everything. He checked the alleyways that he might need to use for entering and exiting the area along with the obstacles that could potentially hinder or aid his movement. As he approached the intersection fifty metres ahead, he knew that turning left onto Jidsuwan Road would lead him to the Aran Gem Gallery, two hundred metres ahead.

Turning the corner and walking along the left-hand side of Jidsuwan Road, Devereaux unfolded a tourist map, periodically stopping as if to check it and using the excuse to survey his surrounds. With his backpack on over his ragged jeans and t-shirt, he looked the part of a tourist, the type that often explored the border town. The pedestrians walked by on either side of the street, going about their business. A Tuk-Tuk driver, asleep in the back of his 'limo', was snoring, the sounds from the street bearly registering or disturbing him.

One hundred metres on the right stood the Aran Gem Gallery, his target location. On the left side, he saw a restaurant. He made his way along the sidewalk, careful not to trip on the uneven pavers that now had an undulation to them. No doubt from heavy tropical rains and a lack of money for repair – it was quite evident that maintenance was not a priority in Aranyaprethet.

As he approached the restaurant, he covertly observed the gallery.

The entrance had a double glass door with chocolate-coloured doorframes. Above the door was a sign made of wood with the name of the store carved in Sanskrit and painted in gold. The façade was made of thin terracotta brick surrounding two large windows.

A stone water feature to the right of the main doors boasted an intricate statue of Buddha as the central piece. The Gallery itself had a tin roof.

There was a light inside, but the windows were tinted, and it was hard to see the interior clearly, however, the vague impression of counters and a doorway could be seen.

Devereaux noted that the street lighting in front of the gallery was non-existent. The only light was to the right side of the building, emanating from a small, low watt fluorescent globe.

Devereaux entered the 'Thai Baan' (Thai House) restaurant, a very bare establishment. Ten plastic tables with seating for four at each table adorned this fine eating establishment, the furnishings more suitable for outdoor dining than in a restaurant. The floor was made of concrete that had been painted with white and orange stripes. The façade was antique Thai. Carved Teakwood with ornate patterns that were painted in a burnt red finish with gold paint trim.

He made his way to the right side of the restaurant, which was three table rows back from the entrance. Pulling out his blue plastic chair, he sat down and placed his backpack next to him on the left. There were two other couples in the restaurant, busily eating away and barely giving Devereaux a second glance as he passed them on the way to his table.

He picked up the menu and started reading through it, looking up and observing the gallery across the road and then returning his gaze to the menu. He looked into his backpack and retrieved a book, a Lonely Planet book, entitled THAILAND. He placed it on the table next to his map and then looked up, beckoning the waitress.

He ordered a coffee and some Pad Thai, Thailand's famous stir- fried noodles. As the waitress moved away, he noticed one of the couples get up and move to the cashier, a dozy old man almost overcome with sleep and inconvenienced by the couple wishing to pay. Not soon after, the second couple left, interrupting the old man once again, his lifeless face emitting no expression, his hands moving as if on automatic pilot. He gave the change to the couple, and the old man slid back into his chair and closed his eyes – not a word was uttered.

Glancing up, Devereaux could see a silhouette moving in the gallery – a woman, he thought.

The silhouette seemed to walk from a doorway on the right side of the counter, perhaps a doorway that led out to the rear of the gallery. The figure walked toward the entrance, and eventually, the glass door opened, and the woman appeared.

She stepped out of the store and closed the door behind her. Her tall body was slim but athletic, long black hair cascading over her shoulders and falling halfway to her waist. She was stunningly beautiful, even in this light.

She made her way across the street and into the Thai Baan, stopping at a table and picked up the menu. She scanned through the list of tasty morsels, then looked around the restaurant and then made eye contact with Devereaux. She made her way to his table and said in perfect American English, 'you look lonely sitting here by yourself' smiling warmly at him.

'What brings you to Aran?'

'Hi' Devereaux replied as he admired her beauty. 'I'm just touring around on my way to Angkor Wat and wanted to experience some Thai country life before heading off' he answered.

'Sorry, wait one minute' she said and turned to the waitress to order her food. Devereaux noted that she ordered enough for at least four people. Was that the number of people currently in the Gallery? He pondered to himself.

'What's your name?' she asked as she turned back around.

'John' he replied. 'And yours?'

'Michelle' she responded, reaching out to shake his hand. Devereaux took her hand and returning the shake, her grip firm echoing an attempted superiority.

'All my friends call me Michelle' she added, with a smile that would melt any mere mortal.

'Nice grip Michelle' Devereaux said, returning the smile.

'May I join you while my food is being prepared?' she asked. 'Sure, grab a seat'. 'Do I hear a hint of a U.S. accent?'

'Yes, I grew up in Los Angeles' she said as she looked at Devereaux contently, a hint of flirtation in her eyes.

'You're from New Zealand, right?' she asked.

'Close, I'm from Sydney' he responded.

'Have you been to Angkor Wat before?'

'No, this is the first time and to be honest, I can't wait.' 'You'll love it! It's thousands of years old, and the architecture will blow your mind. I wish I were going with you – I've visited Angkor several times and never get sick of it' she said.

Devereaux studied her intently as she spoke. Her perfectly shaped eyes and lips provided her face with such animation, the type that attracted people naturally. She was disarming, but Devereaux was not so easily manipulated. He had been manipulated by many a woman, yet none so perfectly sculpted as Michelle if that was her name at all. There was something about her, something that he couldn't quite put his finger on.

Devereaux's food arrived, and the waitress said to the woman, 'one minute, ok?' Indicating her food was almost done.

'Would you like to try?'

'Thanks, but I have an order, it shouldn't be long now. So, how are you finding Aran?' she asked.

'I love little towns like this! They're so different to Bangkok or the other usual tourist traps. People have been so welcoming here - I love it' he said.

'When are you heading off to Angkor?'

'I haven't decided yet, but most likely Thursday.'

The waitress came to the table and gave Michelle her food in three white plastic bags.

'Well, it's been nice meeting you' she said. 'I have to get the food back to a starving crew, or I will be in trouble' she added as she stood and reached out to shake his hand. 'I hope to meet you again sometime!' she said with a blinding smile as she turned and walked away.

Devereaux knew who she was now – Anchalee. The photo he had seen was of a much younger woman, but there was no doubt that this was Getti's daughter.

As she reached the curb and prepared to cross the road, the woman looked over her shoulder back at Devereaux and gave a winning smirk as she caught him still looking at her. He smiled and then looked down, eating his food and glancing up casually from time to time, but not always over at the gallery.

After finishing his meal, Devereaux stood, placed his backpack on his back and walked over to the counter. He put the map on the counter and asked the old man where the railway station was. The man gestured outside and to the right, and the question itself offered Devereaux the cover of an innocently curious tourist rather than the skilled agent he really was. Devereaux's actions were to set up a legitimate question so that if someone was to ask, particularly those across the street, as it was not an unusual question for a tourist to be asking. Devereaux arrived back at his hotel a short while later. The Inn Pound Hotel was located 1.8 kilometres north of the town. As he was dropped off by a Tuk-Tuk, he looked over to the car park and saw his Toyota parked as he requested.

The driver had parked it under a large Mango tree, which provided some cover of darkness for him to retrieve the car keys later on.

The Inn Pound Hotel was the largest in Aranyaprethet. Its street appeal was its huge gable roof held up with four massive white columns. The roof was expansive and covered in terracotta clay tiles. Large windows covered most of the ground floor while on the floor above the main entrance had French windows with reddish-brown timber frames. The hotel was a "U-Shaped" building, with a huge concrete pool situated between the hotel wings.

Devereaux had booked a standard room. A Queen-size bed was central to the room, it had an unimpressive bathroom which had seen better days and the bedroom furnishings were somewhat aged and badly in need of upgrading. All in all, it was perfect for Devereaux and met with his cover story of that as a tourist.

After showering, Devereaux lay on the queen-sized bed and contemplated his day and the encounter with Anchalee. It was a chance encounter, nothing more, but he would have to keep his wits about him from this point on.

There could be nothing left to chance. Tomorrow would see him continue his reconnoitre of the township, particularly that of potential places where he could dump the car after he completed the assassination. He thought about the requirements that would make it look like the killing was a Khmer hit on Getti – a payback for the death of Pim. He would need a place close to the border, near the river, perhaps. That is where he needed to dump the car, or perhaps burn it out and leave signs of Khmer activity – a red and white scarf left on a trail leading to the river's edge would do nicely. Tomorrow, all would be in place.

He switched off the light and laid his head on the pillow to sleep, the USP pistol under his pillow.

Wednesday, 20 February. 20:50hrs

The past two days had been long ones, but Devereaux was finally back at the hotel. Everything he needed to do was completed.

He had watched the Gallery from different vantage points and noticed that the alleyway at the rear of the property was where staff entered and exited.

There had been no sign of Anchalee over the last two days, but there was a vehicle with military numbered plates on it that had stopped briefly in the alleyway for a few minutes and then left along the road system that only had one entry and exit point. From this, he knew the direction in which any vehicle to the rear of the gallery would take.

Devereaux thought that this would be his primary killing area. Devereaux decided to hit the pool for a swim and some badly needed exercise. As he passed through the lobby, he could see some sort of function taking place, some men in military uniform, and others in traditional Thai dress and others, foreigners, dressed in suits.

As he sat on the chair next to the pool, he could hear the music and see people through the window as they celebrated. Devereaux took off his shirt and walked over to the edge of the water, the colour, a brilliant aqua blue as rays of light from the submerged pool lights bounced shimmering light off of its walls.

Diving into the cool water, he began swimming laps up and down the pool. He completed 50 and then swam over to the edge. He placed his forearms on the side of the pool and rested his head, legs floating behind him and eyes closed. He savoured this brief respite from his work for a while, returning to his room feeling invigorated and ready to face the task ahead of him.

He heard footsteps coming from his right side… high heels, he thought. The footsteps stopped in front of him, and he looked up…

Greeting his eyes was that dangerous, yet perfect smile.

'Hey you, I thought it was you, John, how are you?' Michelle said.

'Michelle…hi. What are you doing here?' he replied.

She took off her high heels and pulled up her dress and moved closer to him, sat down in front of him, her thighs either side of his head and lowered her legs into the water. His face only inches away from her panties.

'I see you're not shy' he said and didn't move from his position' she smiled cheekily and said ... 'What would be the point of being bashful when you know what you like?'

'So true' Devereaux replied as his hands slid down and softly grabbed her legs beneath the waterline, his hands feeling her shape.

'I see you are not shy, either' she said.

'That's one thing I have never been accused of' he said with a cheeky smile.

'So, what are you doing here?' he asked.

'Attending a boring function with some guests' she said.

'Hotel guests? Hmmm… I wasn't invited' he replied laughing.

'No silly, guests of the gallery, buyers from Bangkok and Singapore' she added.

'Every quarter, we hold a buyer's event like this. It allows us to show our wares and, with luck, we will get some serious orders' she continued.

'Well I wish you luck tonight' Devereaux replied.

Michelle looked intently at him, a wanting look, and said, 'I think I've already found my luck tonight' as she slid her feet around his back and pulled him closer.

'I'm sure your guests will be missing you... I'm sure a woman of your stature would be well missed' Devereaux said as he looked into her dark eyes.

'In fact, I am sure they are watching us now' he added. 'I can't think of anything more desirable than to spend time with you...alas, my wife would not be amused.' he said.

She looked at him, her feet holding him firmer.

'She is a lucky woman' she said with disappointment, but her eyes said something different, something unbeaten.

She released her grip and Devereaux floated free. Her legs still wide apart, beckoning his attention. Her g-sting was, and he could see a perfect shape through the slightly transparent material, no hair, perfectly shaved. Devereaux's gaze broke with her G-string and then shifted up to her eyes. That devilish smile was like a Siren, beckoning soul. She was trouble!

It was 12:30am, and Devereaux had fallen asleep. His room still as light filtered through the window. A soft knock on the door, Devereaux sat up, took hold of his USP pistol and went to the door, the gun pressed up against the door. As he looked through the peephole, he could see it was Michelle.

'Just a minute' he said. As he turned and slid the pistol under his mattress, positioning the pistol grip just under the mattress for ease of access. He went back to the door, peered out once again and opened the door. Devereaux dressed only in boxer shorts.

'May I?' she said, and walked in, not waiting for approval.

Devereaux looked intently as she walked in, her eyes locked with his.

As she walked passed, she took his hand and led him towards the bed; Devereaux pushing the door closed behind him and flicking the metal latch across to lock the door. His senses were on heightened alert, for he was about to dance with the devil's daughter. She pushed him against the wall, her hands surveying his chest, her eyes doing the same.

He placed his hands on her waist and pulled her close, kissing her hard on her lips, his hands exploring her body, not to examine her shape or for passion, but for weapons.

Their kiss was electric, passionate and deliberate.

Their tongues exploring each other's mouth and their hands caressing each other's bodies.

As they kissed, Devereaux skilfully started undoing the zipper on her skirt, and he allowed the skirt to fall to the floor around her ankles, she flicked it away with her high heels and lowered her hand to caress his manhood through his boxer shorts; he was fully erect.

She undid the buttons on her blouse and slipped it off of her shoulder, the sheer white silk blouse fell away and glided effortlessly to the ground. Devereaux reached down and placed his right arm under her knees and picked her up off the ground and carried her to the bed, she, kissing him as he carried her.

Placing her down on the bed, Devereaux knelt before her and began kissing the inside of her thigh, her transparent G-string now moist and glistening with her flow.

His tongue teasing her as she lay there, her legs open, her back starting to arch as she grabbed his hair, pulling him harder into her. He was relentless with her, teasing her until she came to the edge of climax and then he stopped.

He was in control.

She reached down to pull him up and onto her, but he grabbed her wrists and pinned them to the bed. He started his tease all over again, bringing her to the edge of climax, then letting her subside again. Each time he repeated the tease until she could bear it no more - her back arching hard and her body shaking as his tongue brought her to a hard, shuddering climax. Devereaux, still holding her wrists down, looked up and he could see the beads of sweat trickling down her well-formed breasts and onto her flat stomach. Her breathing was heavy, but she was recovering well. She twisted her wrists to the side and pulled him forward and up onto the bed.

'Fuck you' she said...

'You don't control me' she added with conviction, 'I control you!'

And with that, she straddled him guiding his member deep inside her and began her rhythmic dance. Pleasuring herself as she gradually moved faster and with more aggression. He placed his hands on her waist, and she immediately pushed them away, slapping his face and saying:

'I didn't say you could touch me,' and she thrust her pelvis back hard, showing him she was the one in control. He thrust up hard into her, and she reached down and grabbed his throat with her hand, squeezing her hand tight as she continued to rock back and forth on his manhood.

Devereaux flexing his neck muscles until she finally let go for a second time, her climax as powerful as her first; Devereaux still flexing his neck muscles to counter her grip. She started to moan as she slowed her rhythmic gyrations.

Devereaux was having none of it and gave her no time to recover. He rolled his body to the side, forcing her from him and turned her onto her stomach and held her down by the back of the neck, his other hand placing a large pillow under her hips and he mounted her and controlled her. She bucked back and tried to regain dominance, as Devereaux entered her and thrust hard and deeper inside - her body stopped its effort to regain control as a second more powerful thrust followed.

Grabbing her long black hair, he pulled it back and slightly to the right so that her head was tilted to one side, so she could see him thrusting into her from behind. He pushed deeper inside her once again and said:

'No one controls me, you are mine to have, how I want,' and he began to thrust harder and faster, repeating it over and over until he ejaculated forcefully inside her. Both collapsing on the bed next to each other - both spent and dripping with sweat.

After a few minutes, Michelle got up and walked around to the end of the bed. Looking at Devereaux, she smiled and reached down and picked up her skirt, put it on and then her bra and silk blouse. Devereaux watched every move she made, her eyes always looking at him with a defiant manner. She sat on the bed and put on her high heel shoes, stood and walked around to Devereaux and leaned forward and kissed him passionately and then breathed out a heavy breath. Taking him by the hand, still naked, she walked him over to the door and kissed him hard once more, then slapped his face in defiance. He pushed her against the door and kissed her hard again, this time she smiled, and she turned and opened the door and without a word, left, and he closed and locked the door behind her. Devereaux walked back to the bed, retrieving the pistol and placing it next to him.

Thursday, 21 February. 10:09hrs

Devereaux eased the brakes on the white Toyota as he approached the intersection of highway 33 and 384, a kilometre from the Inn Pound Hotel. As the Toyota stopped, a man approached the driver's side window and knocked on it. It was a street vendor, and he tapped on the window again to get Devereaux's attention. The vendor, wearing a blue baseball cap, reached up and grasped the peak of the cap and swung it around so that the peak was to the rear, and tapped on the window once again.

Devereaux looked again at the vendor and opened the window, the vendor going into full flight with his sales pitch, his aim to sell the bags of peanuts and bottles of water. Devereaux relented, saying, 'Ok, Ok, peanut and water', handing the man 20Baht. The vendor handed a bottle of water to Devereaux and dropped the bag of peanuts in his lap. The traffic lights changed to green and Devereaux accelerated away from the vendor, leaving him to haggle his wares with another driver.

With that, the brush contact was over. The vendor was an agent sent to deliver a message from Connor. The vendor's safety signal was to turn the peak of his cap to the rear, indicating it was safe to make contact.

Devereaux's counter signal was to roll down his window. The contact had to look as natural as possible and something that was well in place with the environment. On the pack of the peanuts was a white label, a Red Elephant was stamped on the label, and an innocuous product packing number was placed in the bottom right-hand corner: B2221c.

Devereaux deciphered the code: the "B" meaning BRIMSTONE, the "22" meaning the date – the 22nd, the "21" meaning 2100hrs and the "c" meaning confirmed.

Devereaux now had confirmation that Getti would be at the designated location on Friday at 21:00hrs.

CHAPTER 17

'The Sanction'

ARANYAPRETHET, THAILAND

Friday. 20:03hrs

From all intelligence reports, General Sompon Getti would visit the Aran Gem Gallery today. He used an old 1967 Mercedes Benz when he was in Aran, the pearl white coat on the vehicle immaculate. Devereaux had scouted Aran for the past five days. He knew every way to approach the Gallery, the entry point that Getti would use, and where he would park his vehicle. He knew the various vantage points and the location in which he could immobilise the General's car and, ultimately, engage Getti himself.

Earlier in the week, Devereaux had found a suitable place where he could dump the vehicle after the hit. The location was off of highway 4001, 12kms south of Aran and a further 7kms east of Khlong Nam Sai village.

The location he had chosen was literally in the middle of a rural area with no housing for at least 3kms in any direction, and it was located right on the Thai-Cambodian border; the border being a river that ran east-west. He had cachéd his motorcycle there earlier in the day.

Two kilometres northwest of the caché site was a small surveying company, "Thai Aerial Survey". The company had two UH1H Huey helicopters in their compound that were used for surveying the border areas in addition to general surveying of potential mineral deposits. Devereaux had noted earlier in the day, as he passed the compound, that one of the Huey's was being refuelled while the other remained parked with no human interaction happening around it.

The Hueys were almost surely Vietnam War leftovers that had once belonged to the infamous CIA run "Air America", a service that operated predominantly in Laos during the war.

They were even still painted in the typical Air America livery of Blue and White.

The rain had started to fall more substantially, but it was intermittent. The windscreen wipers did their best on high speed to clear the windscreen but were not as effective as they might have been thanks to the furore with which the heavy tropical raindrops smashed against the glass. The weather was perfect, Devereaux thought, as it would keep most people indoors and off the streets. He steered the car to the left and gently applied the brakes, bringing the Toyota to a halt and parking it on the side of the road. He switched off the engine and looked around the area. It was quiet, the street was poorly lit, but he could see a few people out on the road scampering to get out of the rain. Before exiting the car, he reached up and made sure the interior light switch was in the "off" position so that when he exited the vehicle – and, more importantly, when he returned – the interior light would not be activated, allowing him to operate in shadow.

He exited the car, grabbing a large bag from the back seat as he did so, and headed off down the dimly lit street in the rain after locking the car door. 150 metres later, he turned down a narrow side street. Another 50 metres further and he entered an alleyway that led to his chosen firing destination. Yesterday, Devereaux had found an abandoned, partially burnt outbuilding that looked straight down the narrow road behind the gallery where Getti would have to park his car. The road was sealed, but had been neglected for some time and was riddled with potholes that had now filled with water. The road was directly behind the gallery and provided access to buildings in the area. Devereaux had decided that the old house was the perfect location from which to fire the RPG-7. The position was slightly elevated, and his target would be about one hundred metres away. With the RPG optical sight attached, and utilising the illuminated reticule, he would have no difficulty hitting the target with the first grenade, as he was already highly proficient with the weapon. Behind where the vehicle would be parked, a streetlight that emitted a soft amber glow, perfect for silhouettes to be painted against.

20:25hrs

Devereaux entered the burnt-out building from a small laneway that cut through the neighbourhood. He carefully pulled back on a section of broken mesh wire on a fence that attempted to secure the property.

Slipping through the opening, he walked cautiously through the rubble and up the concrete staircase to the first floor. He entered the charred remains of what was once a large master bedroom. Two large floor-to-ceiling windows looked out to the street below. Taking up a position that was two metres back from the window, he remained in the shadows, taking care to stay back from the window itself. His chosen position in the darkness was perfect. He lowered his kit bag silently and knelt next to it, looking out the window and down at the rear entrance to the gallery.

'What the fuck!' Devereaux muttered to himself.

Getti's Mercedes was already parked in position at the rear of the Gallery. Of all days, the devil had to be early.

He had no time to waste, he wasn't sure how long Getti had been in the Gallery or when he might decide to leave. He quickly unzipped his kitbag, pulled out the RPG-7 and laid it next to him. Then, he took out two PG-7VL HEAT Grenades and two boosters and began screwing the boosters to the sustainer motors.

The booster rocket would launch the grenade out of the RPG-7 tube and the inertia of high g-forces on the warhead would arm the sustainer motor, fuse and self-destruct mechanisms. By the time the grenade reached Getti's vehicle, the warhead would be ready for business.

Devereaux placed the RPG on his shoulder, turned on the sight illumination system and looked through the eyepiece. The vehicle was illuminated perfectly, and the soft amber light behind the vehicle provided the sighting system with good, clear visibility. He looked carefully at the vehicle, and a sudden movement caught his eye – the driver was seated behind the wheel, his arm hanging outside the window and a cigarette clenched between his fingers. The vehicle was facing forward towards Devereaux, a fact that he would have to live with. When the driver started the car, headlights would flood the ground floor of the building. Devereaux would need to factor that into the equation when firing.

Devereaux removed the AK-M assault rifle from his bag, place a 30 round magazine on the weapon and cocked it. He taped an additional 30 round magazine to the one already on the weapon, allowing for a quick magazine change. The AK-M and the RPG would be left in place. He reached into the bag and removed a red and white scarf, typical of Khmer clothing.

It was soiled and old. He would leave it attached to the wire by the fence on his way out, a tell-tale sign and a hint of a Khmer reprisal. He placed the RPG back on his shoulder, scanning the area with the optics.

A light from behind the Gallery was turned on, but the light didn't travel past the back gate making the area rather dark. All of a sudden, the back gate opened. People quickly gathered near the car, and the driver immediately threw his cigarette out of the window to get out and open the rear passenger door. It was Getti.

The rain had eased, but the cluster of people was eager to get out of the now drizzling rain that was persistently falling. Getti quickly shook hands with two people that were obscured in shadow, and then he turned and entered the vehicle. Devereaux placed his thumb on the cocking mechanism of the RPG, readying it to fire. He had one chance and one chance only.

Just as he lined up the sights, a third-person darted out from the shadows and entered the car, but he was unable to see who it was.

As the driver hurriedly returned to the other side of the vehicle and opened the driver's door, a man on a motorcycle rode up next to the Mercedes and stopped level with the rear door and waited. Devereaux had not seen this rider; he was parked in the shadows under a twenty-meter Mango tree. An army bodyguard he thought… possibly, but that didn't matter right now, the target was Getti. Devereaux took aim, and as the driver entered the car, Devereaux fired the RPG. The rocket booster ignited, thrusting the grenade out of the tube and within a second, the warhead had struck its target, the grenade piercing the central lower edge of the windscreen and exploding inside of the vehicle.

The shock wave was felt by Devereaux seventy metres away.

As the grenade exploded, a fireball consumed the inside of the vehicle and fragmentation spread through the occupants. The motorcycle rider, who had pulled up next to the car at the last minute, was blown off the motorcycle entirely, his body flying through the air like a rag doll before slamming into a fence. The rider, crumpled in a heap on the ground, his left sleeve on fire.

Devereaux quickly reloaded the RPG, aimed and fired the second rocket into the car. Another loud explosion rocked the vehicle, lifting it partially off the ground. The fuel tank erupted, and the car was engulfed in a merciless fire.

He dropped the RPG, took up the AK-M and fired 30 rounds into the vehicle, aiming particularly where he saw Getti getting into the car.

He quickly changed magazines and fired another 30 rounds into the vehicle, before dumping the AK on the ground. Devereaux looked at the car; it was a mass of flames, fuelled by a ruptured fuel tank. He could see bodies burning inside.

Devereaux, staying in a crouched position, moved towards the stairway, the kit bag across his back.

Exiting the building, he moved over toward the fence, placing the red and white checked scarf on a sharp piece of wire as though it got caught as the assailant departed the area.

He passed through the gap and made his way along the laneway, staying in the shadows as he made his way to his vehicle. He walked casually along the dark road towards his car, maintaining vigilance along the way.

Sirens in the distance started to pierce the night air as the rain began to pour once again. Devereaux had calculated that the best possible delay for emergency services to get to the area would be 8 minutes, and now that it had started to rain heavily, it would add another 1-2 minutes onto that time.

Arriving at his car, he quickly opened the door and threw his bag across to the passenger seat, hopped in and closed the door behind him. He started the engine and pulled away from the parking lot. He didn't turn on any lights until about five hundred metres from the parking area as he made his way to highway 4001.

Getti's car continued to burn. Against the fence, a seemingly lifeless body moved. The small finger on the left hand curled up then straightened out again, followed by the remaining fingers. The head encased in a black helmet started to move slowly from side to side as the rider began to come to. The right arm moved anchored itself on the ground as he tried to get himself up on to his feet. As he rose, he collapsed to the ground again and lay there for a minute before trying once again.

This time he made it to his knees, his right arm moving across and grasping his left arm. A shard of metal pierced his bicep and protruded from his black jacket. His helmet pocked with tiny fragments of glass, a laceration to his right shoulder where he hit some jagged tin when he was flung off his motorcycle and into the fence.

He lifted his visor, the helmet was studded with debris and looked at the car, the three burning corpses laid to waste in the vehicle. He fell back to his knees and screamed in horror, 'FATHER!'

Devereaux drove at normal speed away from the site and was now four kilometres away. In the distance, he could see the dull glow of the fire and the flashing of red lights emanating from emergency services vehicles as they approached the carnage.

The rain stopped as quickly as it had come. The clouds seemed to have parted, and he could see moonlight streaming through.

Devereaux knew he had a long way to go before he was safe, but he was satisfied at a job well done all the same.

CHAPTER 18

'Exfiltration'

ARANYAPRETHET, THAILAND

02:25hrs

It took Devereaux longer than expected to dump his vehicle. He decided to execute a deception plan by circling back along part of the route he had already taken to see if he was being followed. He finally arrived at the site and parked the vehicle just short of the location itself.

He killed the lights and stepped outside the car, walking two hundred metres to the location he had chosen. The moon was at its waning quarter and glowed through the broken clouds above making visibility acceptable.

Devereaux squatted and used a small pair of binoculars to scan the area. He stood slowly and moved towards the area where he had cachéd his motorcycle; stopping once more to scan the area as he got closer.

He started to remove the camouflage from the motorcycle and pushed it out into the cleared area, placed the stand down and returned to his car. He stopped next to the vehicle and listened. He could hear vehicles off in the distance – a long way from his present location. He eased himself back into the car and drove to the edge of the river where his motorcycle was parked. He began winding down all of the windows in the car and found a solid piece of wood that he could use to hold down the accelerator pedal. All unnecessary equipment was placed inside his kit bag and then lashed to the seat with the seat belt woven through the kit bag handles, preventing anything from floating to the surface.

With the engine still running, Devereaux jammed the piece of wood between the seat and the accelerator causing the vehicle to rev noisily, he put it in gear and the car surged forward as Devereaux leapt free as it was propelled into the river. The Toyota began to submerge as the water filled the interior of the vehicle, the hiss of air bubbles purging as the vehicle finally found its watery grave.

03:59hrs

Devereaux walked to his motorcycle and stood quietly, listening once again. He could hear an engine purring – it was coming from the river. He looked to the east and could see a beam of light hitting the water and searching the banks.

Devereaux was in the open – if he didn't move, he would definitely be seen. He quickly accelerated away from the bank, but the searchlight, coming from a military river patrol boat, changed to follow the noise on the Thai side of the border.

The searchlight scanned from left to right and finally found its prey. It followed Devereaux as he desperately tried to getaway.

A voice over a loudspeaker ordered the motorcyclist to stop, but it kept moving, changing direction and accelerating away from the river. A burst of machine-gun fire tore up the ground to his right. Turning the bike to the left, he opened the throttle and finally escaped, changing direction again. He had broken contact for now, and he eased back on the throttle only to find that the bike started to slow faster than expected and eventually came to a halt.

Devereaux lowered the motorcycle on its side in the middle of a paddy field to keep a low profile. He looked down at the gearbox next to the pedals and saw a hole in it. A round fired from the machine gun narrowly missing Devereaux's left leg had pierced the gearbox; the motorcycle would go no further. Devereaux was on foot and on the move. He knew he had to put as much distance between himself and the river as possible. In the distance, he could hear faint sirens – police or military, he thought to himself. He had to get moving. He started running to the northwest and, he needed to get away from the area as quickly as possible or risk being captured. He remembered that the Thai Aerial Survey compound was not that far away – at most, one kilometre from his current location. He picked up the pace, crossing the open padi fields and stopping every two hundred metres to listen.

On his feet again - running - larger paces now; changing direction and then changing again. More gunfire - this time, but further away.

They had lost him, but the sirens were getting closer.

The net was getting tighter.

He could see the compound and the silhouette of the Huey. That was it, his way out!

Devereaux made it to the compound, and, using the shadows, skirted around until he was directly adjacent to the Huey he had seen being refuelled earlier that day. He could hear the sirens, but they seemed to be going further south. Devereaux unlashed the rotor holds attached to the tail boom and to the tip of the rotor, allowing the rotor to move freely to the horizontal position above the fuselage.

He raced around to the front right-hand door, opened it and climbed in.

Reaching up to the overhead console, he used the palm of his hand and made sure that all the fuses were pushed in.

Moving further forward on the console, he flicked the battery switch to the "ON" position, and a hum started to emanate as the Huey was awoken from its slumber.

He looked out the window and could see red and blue flashing lights getting closer.

No time to waste!

Looking down to the centre console he switched the hydraulics to ON.

Then, the Force Trim button was switched to ON.

He then pushed both the Fuel button and the Fuel Start buttons forward to ON.

Directly below the Fuel Start button was the Fuel Pump switch, which he also pushed forward to the ON position.

As he looked out through the windows to scan the area, he reached down to the left side of his seat and located the "Collective" lever, which controlled the helicopters vertical movement. On the collective lever was the throttle. Devereaux twisted the throttle counter-clockwise to the fully wide-open position. Looking up at the volts meter, he could see it was at 24.5 volts, which was low, but adequate for a start. Devereaux readied the craft for take-off and pressed the Start Ignition Trigger Switch.

The engine started to come to life, and the rotors began turning.

He reached down again to the centre console and switched off the "Start Fuel" button to prevent excess fuel from being pumped into the engine.

He reached up to the overhead console again and switched the Inverters "ON" and the Auto Electrics.

Rotors now at full RPM and he eased back on the throttle.

Looking out of the windows, he could see a police car approaching, less than two hundred metres away and closing the distance fast.

A sudden crack and a bullet pierced the co-pilot's window and went out through the front windshield. Devereaux rolled back the throttle to full power and started to pull up on the Collective, and pushed slightly on the left pedal to counter the torque while keeping the fuselage from spinning under the rotor disc.

Another round entered the rear passenger door and passed through the Huey and out through the other rear door.

Devereaux pushed forward on the Cyclic, the control stick positioned between the pilot's legs and controlled the Huey's forward, rear and sideways movements, and he pushed forward in a controlled and firm manner to prepare to perform a "Hot" take off.

The chopper rolled forward and climbed to an altitude of sixty metres, and, as the Huey picked up speed, Devereaux eased the cyclic over to the right, pushing on the right pedal at the same time, causing the Huey to bank to the right. He headed at low-level due west for approximately five minutes. He began to bank the Huey to the left and headed due south and over the border into Cambodia, maintaining a heading of 180° for 10 minutes. Devereaux eased the throttle back to maintain the ideal power and rotated the Power Control Friction Adjuster just above the throttle to lock the throttle setting.

He nudged the cyclic forward until the speed indicator showed a cruising speed of 120kts. He pulled up slightly on the collective so that he was sixty metres above the ground to avoid any trees or power lines that may be in the area, the moonlight allowing him to see the changes in the terrain below. Devereaux searched around for a map. He found one shoved in the pilot's door by his right leg. Retrieving it, he was initially disappointed to see it marred with a dark liquid. He turned on the map light and saw it was blood… his blood! Looking up and checking that the aircraft was level and the altitude was ok, he reached down and felt his calf muscle and was instantly rewarded with a hot, stinging pain.

Pulling up his jeans, Devereaux saw a graze from one of the rounds on his calf. Where the round itself ended up was a mystery. He hadn't felt it hit – his adrenalin levels must have masked the pain. Checking the aircraft attitude once again, he looked over his right shoulder and saw, attached to a pillar of the fuselage was a medkit.

He ripped it free and took out a bandage, wrapped it around the small wound and tightly strapped it to prevent more bleeding.

Devereaux realised he was lucky to escape with just a scratch.

Looking at the map, he picked a location, 40 Nautical Miles (NM) north of Phnom Penh. It was 153NM from Aran to a potential landing ground, and he had calculated that travelling at 120kts it would take him 1hour, 16minutes.

He reached forward and set the compass to 125° and banked the Huey to match the course required and concentrated on keeping the aircraft flying on heading. He glanced at the fuel instrument, and the aircraft was full, more than enough fuel to get to the desired LZ as he was carrying no cargo and the Huey was travelling light.

The route he had hastily planned would see him fly 8kms to the north of Battambang, controlled airspace.

He would use the mountain range to mask his presence and fly as low as possible through that region until he can find a passage through the mountain and to the Tonle Sap Lake.

He would stay amongst the rain forest that follows the Tonle Sap.

He would be able to fly at treetop level from there avoiding any air traffic control and hopefully find an LZ without detection. From there it would be on foot and a river taxi ride into Phnom Penh.

Devereaux reached inside his shirt and pulled out his USP pistol and began stripping it. He slid the window open and started to throw pieces out of the window as he flew along – first the magazines, the silencer, the slide and then the pistol grip assembly. Devereaux was now weaponless, a strange, naked feeling considering the past 24 hours.

Devereaux could see the dawn approaching. It was now 04:45hrs and he could see the mountain range north of Battambang. He pushed down on the collective to lower the altitude of the chopper and was now flying nape-of-the-earth, skimming just above the trees for as long as possible. The dawn light allowed him to bring the aircraft as close as possible to the mountains, contouring them and masking the aircraft from detection.

Ahead, he could see a pass through the mountains that would bring him into a position near the Tonle Sap, and, eventually to the Tonle Sap Delta where he would find a place to land.

The shimmer of the dawn light on the lake was comforting to Devereaux, and he quietly pondered the last 24 hours. He had completed the mission of terminating Getti but thought about the two other poor bastards in the car, not to mention the guy on the motorcycle. They had paid with their lives, and for what?

He had 16 minutes to run before he needed to find a landing zone. Devereaux checked the map and found a location that looked suitable; just how suitable, he wouldn't know until he was overhead. He could see the location on the map, in between two small rainforest-covered hills, which met with some grassland. At first sight, it looked perfect, but as Devereaux brought the aircraft in closer, he could see there was some secondary growth – saplings up to three metres in height. There was no time to waste, he needed to get the chopper down before the region became too busy. He decided to go for the LZ and banked the Huey steeply to the right and made a final approach.

The chopper was five metres above the ground as Devereaux brought it into a hover and did one final check before sinking the Huey lower and lower towards the ground until the skids of the Huey made contact.

Devereaux eased back on the throttle until it was at the idle position and commenced the shutdown procedure and the bird fell quiet. He opened the door and began to wipe down the blood that was on the inside of the door and the floor. He bent down to pick up some soil and rubbed it into the blood spots and then washed it down with some water, removing any sign that it ever existed.

Devereaux found some foliage and hastily camouflaged the Huey just to make it a bit more challenging to spot. The three-meter saplings, he had mowed down with the rotors were ideal as they were heavy with leaves.

Devereaux had been walking through the mountains for an hour. The LZ Devereaux had chosen proved to be the right location as there seemed to be limited access to the site. He had made it to a road and, by his reckoning, he was 2km south of the village of Kaoh K'Aek and 42km north of Phnom Penh.

The road he found was heading downhill and towards a watercourse that flowed from the Tonle Sap Lake, which would eventually lead him all the way into the city. Waiting at a small jetty, he saw an orange and blue river taxi approaching. He waved to it and the boat veered course and came alongside.

'Phnom Penh?' Devereaux asked. The coxswain nodded his head in the affirmative.

Devereaux had no Cambodian Riel and handed the man US$20. The man smiled widely and said, 'thank you, mister' and laughed, knowing he had been given way too much.

Devereaux returned the smile and sat just in front of the coxswain. The man tapped Devereaux on the shoulder and pointed to his leg that was still bleeding, the man's gesture asking what happened.

'Dog' Devereaux replied, but the man looked confused.

'Dog – woof-woof!' Devereaux exclaimed, holding his hand up, the fingers imitating the jaw and teeth of a mangy mutt biting his leg. The man laughed and shook his head, slapping Devereaux's shoulder in amusement of the tourist's plight.

The water taxi had some grunt, pushing a respectable speed and was making good time as it hurtled along the river. It's hefty V-8 engine capable of propelling the water taxi, fully loaded, easily at 60kms per hour. At this rate, he'd be in Phnom Penh within the hour.

Devereaux took in the scenery as they raced along the waterway and felt a calmness come over him. As the landscape passed by, he was considering his next move.

The water taxi pulled up alongside a riverbank, the coxswain shouting to Devereaux, 'Phnom Penh, mister'. Devereaux placed his small pack over his shoulder and stood, thanking the man as he disembarked the vessel and made his way to the street. The bustling city was a far cry from the sleepy Aran, he thought, as he scanned the area, an old habit that seemed to never die.

Looking up, he saw a blue and white street sign that read, 130 Street.

Looking left and right, he hustled across the road, dodging the chaotic traffic. As he walked along 130 Street, he found a store selling cheap jeans and shirts.

He waded through to find jeans that were European size. 34", he chuckled to himself. 'Perfect!' They were 501-Levi Strauss jeans, basic, but at US$20, what the hell. As he walked to the cashier counter, he took a dark blue Polo Shirt off of the rack and glanced at the size, "L", and then placed it across the crook of his arm and proceeded to the checkout. The young lady put the clothes in a bag and said $25. A bargain at any price, Devereaux thought.

Five hundred metres up 130 Street; the street widened and became Khemarak Phomin. As Devereaux walked toward the Central Market building some four hundred metres ahead, he looked to his left and saw a pharmacy. He needed supplies to fix his leg, he thought, before infection set in. After buying some antibiotics, some fresh bandages and cleaning agents, he exited the pharmacy and looked for a safe place to rest. Fifty metres ahead, he saw a small hotel, the "Frangipani Hotel". It was old but looked well maintained and hinted of old colonial French architecture. Entering the foyer, he walked over to the reception where a woman in her 30s glanced up with a welcoming smile.

'Good morning sir, may I help you?' she asked.

'I would like a room for the day, please' he replied.

'May I see your passport, sir?' she requested.

Devereaux reached into his pack and handed her a passport.

'Mr. Smith – Mr. John Smith?' the woman said.

'Yes. Do you have a room with a bath by any chance?' Devereaux asked.

'Yes, Mr. Smith, we have a suite available on the top floor. It has a large bath and large bed' she added.

'How much is it for the day?'

'It's US$150, would you like it?' she asked.

'Yes, thank you' he said, and handed $150 across the counter. Devereaux picked up his passport and placed it in his front pocket, took the key to the room and headed upstairs.

The room was huge and had high ceilings. It had white cornices and cream coloured walls. A large antique bed with beautiful linen was the pride of the room. The bathroom had a vintage Cheviot Regal cast iron tub atop four clawfoot brass bathtub feet. It was just what Devereaux needed. For the next hour, Devereaux soaked his body in the hot bath, his wound seeping tiny traces of blood into the water.

After he finished, he cleaned the wound thoroughly and applied antiseptic ointment and a clean dressing. He changed into his new clothes and collected all the waste bandages and placed them into a plastic bag. He then double-checked the room to ensure nothing was left behind and preceded downstairs and out onto the street, where he hailed a taxi to go to the airport. The road was congested, but the traffic was moving ok.

He arrived at the airport and immediately went to a ticket booth to see if there were any flights to Sydney that afternoon.

The man behind the counter, 20 to 25 years of age looked intently at the screen and said 'there is a flight at 3:00pm today on Qantas, it's a direct flight, but unfortunately there are no seats available' he said. Then he held up his hand and said, 'No, wait, sir, I'm sorry, there are two seats available, but they are business class. The cost is US$1,200 for a one-way ticket.'

'Wow, that's so expensive!' Devereaux exclaimed, but he didn't really care – it was just conversation.

'I'll take it, thanks' he said and handed over the cash for the flight.

There were just 90 minutes to go before his flight departed. Devereaux moved through the passenger terminal after going through immigration and made his way over to the bar area.

He looked up at the large departure screen that indicated his flight would depart on time. A bar was situated close to Devereaux's departure gate, where he sat and watched the TV. There were images of Aranyaprethet and the horrific attack on a senior Defence Force member. No names were given, just the importance of his position. The video images showed a burning car, the glow

281

reflecting off the nearby tin fence, and a motorcycle hardly recognisable lying next to the burning vehicle. Police and military could be seen in the video looking over the scene. The reporter gave no indication as to who committed the crime, only that three were confirmed dead, and the motorcyclist was seriously injured.

Devereaux turned away from the TV and asked the bartender behind the bar for a Singha. A few seconds later, the beer was placed in front of him. He looked across the bar and into a mirror, and raised his beer as if to say 'cheers' to the man in the reflection… "Brimstone" was dead!

CHAPTER 19

'Sydney'

SYDNEY, AUSTRALIA

February. 21:30hrs

Darling Harbour was busy – thousands of people had flocked to the playground on this balmy summer night. Devereaux walked through the crowd along the boardwalk, rainbow-coloured lights from neon signs splashed across the dark water of the harbour, while music poured from the myriad of different bars. Groups of young professionals made their way to the docks, leaving their castles of toil behind for the week, their new missions to enjoy the elixirs of pleasure and forget the nursing of hangovers the next day.

On the left, a paved stairway resembling a mini amphitheatre, a group of teens acting like a congress of baboons skylarked around, half-drunk at this early hour of the night, but not annoying anyone. Their antics were not unnoticed by many, but they brought a smile to Devereaux as he passed and remembered the escapades of his own youth.

He took a set of stairs leading up to the roadway above. At the top of the stairs, a red "flashing man" perched high on the traffic light post, halting the movement of humans from crossing the busy intersection. This gave way to a green glow, and the crowd moved across the road, weaving their way into their own space. Devereaux headed diagonally across the intersection and up the hill along King Street. His destination was P. J. O'Brien's Irish pub at the Grace Hotel.

The Grace Hotel on the corner of King and George Street was a Sydney icon. Built in the 1920s, its magnificent, twelve-storey sandstone structure was the height of opulence in its time. Its spacious rooms, wide stairways and ornate woodwork made the old place permeate wealth and grandeur.

It was a favourite hotel of Devereaux, and when he could, he would always opt to stay there. But not on this trip to Sydney. Today, he was at the Grace Hotel for another purpose.

The Concierge opened the door as Devereaux entered the Grace. The 1920s feel emanated the splendour of the old building – what stories it could tell! During World War II, and, more specifically, during the war in the Pacific, the Grace served as the headquarters of the U.S. armed forces under General Douglas MacArthur. When Devereaux stayed there, he couldn't help conjuring up images that danced through his mind of uniformed 1940's soldiers walking the halls and of General MacArthur's neo-gothic corner office perched high above George Street.

Its art deco style, coupled with dark timber and wrought iron balustrading, gave the old girl a feel of nostalgia. As Devereaux passed the reception desk to his left, the ornate chandeliers cast an auburn glow that was reflected on the tiled floor below. At the end of the corridor was an antique sign hanging high over the heavy wooden doorframe.

Flanked either side of the door were ornate stained-glass windows beckoning passers-by into P.J. O'Brien's. Devereaux pulled back on the solid brass door handles and entered the bar, his eyes and mind taking photographs of the noisy crowd inside. He scanned and calculated the new environment, faces, exits, possible items he could use as weapons, potential threats – his mind was in operational mode once again.

The place was packed, and Devereaux had to turn sideways to make passage through the horde to get to the bar and order his Guinness. While he waited for his order, an Irish band – two men and a woman – played "Ode To My Family". Over the top of the crowd, he saw Connor sitting over in the corner near the street entrance.

His concentration was focused on a newspaper, and without a break in concentration, he held up his index finger gesturing to Devereaux, one for him, too. Devereaux turned back at the barman and asked for one more, smiling at Connor's uncanny sense of surroundings and his timing to avoid paying for the round. Cheap bastard!

Devereaux moved across the dark emerald green carpet toward the table where Connor was seated.

'Great timing' said Devereaux as he placed a Guinness in front of Connor.

'Hand on my heart, I had no idea you were there!' he said with a cheeky smile.

'Spare me' Devereaux started laughing.

'Welcome home, John. Glad you're in one piece' he added.

'Good to be home and back to some sanity' Devereaux replied.

'We have a lot to chat about! When you leave, take this newspaper as it has some info for you' Connor said as he took a large swig of his Guinness. 'Magnus wants us to meet tomorrow – the details are in the notes I have provided to you.'

Connor folded over the newspaper, stood and drank what was left of his Guinness and said, 'When you get back to your hotel, check out Page 3, it's a good read ol' son. Thanks for the drink, see you tomorrow' Connor added, turning and walking away. 'Thanks for returning the shout you cheap bastard' Devereaux said with a smile and shook his head.

Devereaux sat and listened to the music until he had finished his Guinness, then, folding the newspaper tighter, stood with the newspaper under his left arm. He looked down at the table once to ensure nothing was left behind and then walked out onto the street. As he walked along George Street, heading towards Martin Place, he pondered the lives of the people that walked the streets around him. They were totally oblivious to the world around them and what it takes to keep them safe. How could they be so naïve as to what really occurs – what was really necessary to be done, what violence it took to keep them safe? He looked at some young adults walking along the road, some with beer bottles in their hands and others acting like idiots. Why did they care so little and why were they so appalled by men like him, who were willing to commit such violence so they could pursue their seemingly inconsequential lives? At times, Devereaux struggled with such questions. He was never able to produce a significant – or at least a substantive – answer that made his sacrifice worthwhile. Indeed, he thought they were unworthy of his sacrifice.

His room at the Westin Sydney Hotel, on Martin Place, was adequate. The small room was typical for the centre of the CBD, where the guests were mostly travelling businessmen and only needed a place to rest their heads. He would only be there for the next 24 hours before heading back to Queenscliff, where he would have to give some serious consideration to his marriage – if, in fact, that was a decision he had to make at all. Alesha had already moved on, at least mentally.

Lying back on the bed, Devereaux opened the newspaper, flicked through to page three as Connor had suggested, and found a business card. The card was black in colour on one side with the words "Mortimer House" in gold embossed lettering.

The other side of the card was white with a handwritten message in blue ink, the shape of the text indicating a hand skilled at using a fountain pen: "10am – tomorrow – Wear a suit. 127 George Street."

'Shit, a suit' Devereaux mumbled and rolled his eyes. He hated suits – they made him feel like a "has-been", a non-operator, and that just wouldn't do.

Glancing down at the newspaper positioned partway down the page an article caught his eye.

"THE TRIBUNE"

Friday, February 27, 1992

THAI GENERAL MURDERED

BANGKOK, (Reuters). *An enquiry into the 22 February assassination of General Sompon Getti, Thailand's Special Forces Commander, was announced today.*

Gen. Getti was assassinated while on official business in Aranyaprethet. Unknown assailants ambushed him and his daughter, Captain Anchalee Getti when getting into their car.

The incident also saw the death of the General's Aid, Captain Kuchai. Notably, General Getti's son, Major Chatri, was wounded in the attack, suffering burns to his left forearm as well as shrapnel wounds to his arms and legs.

The assailants are believed to have escaped across the border into Cambodia.

The assassination is alleged to have been linked to the illegal gem smuggling trade associated with former Khmer Rouge members formerly headed by the, now deceased, General Dang Pim. General Getti was allegedly implicated in the illicit trade and was under investigation for his complicity. An unnamed source said that the assassination of Getti was a reprisal for Getti's involvement in the murder of General Dang Pim.

Devereaux sat quietly, reading the name "Anchalee" and re-reading that section twice. The shadowy figure that flashed from the darkness into the back seat of the Mercedes, seconds before Devereaux squeezed the trigger, hurtling the rocket to its target. The fiery death bestowed on the woman that he had only days before shared a bed with… gone in an inferno.

'Fuck' he said as he pushed the newspaper away, his blood simmering.

She was not his mission, nor was the general's aid, and yet with ease, he erased them as if they were insignificant.

Devereaux sighed with some remorse yet knew Getti had to be stopped. However, it was an unfortunate collateral incident, and he lamented its occurrence.

Devereaux didn't care for the reason Magnus Webb had given him before sending him on this mission – the UNTAC mission was of no concern to him. The importation of large quantities of heroin into Australia and the effect on the Australian populace was another thing altogether. That was the single most crucial factor to Devereaux; it was worth the cost of the mission.

CHAPTER 20

'Mortimer House'

SYDNEY

10:00hrs

Devereaux walked along the right-hand side of George Street, heading down to the Rocks area. His destination was "Mortimer House." As he approached, he was surprised at the aesthetics and how technical the architectural design was.

The beautiful masonry of the 1882 building, which was once a Police Station, was a prime example of Colonial architecture. Its two-storey façade built almost entirely of sandstone, boasted a huge arch over the entrance stairway, were Lion's head sat as the keystone to the arch, looking down with an air of nobility.

Two columns supported the arch with six square sandstone blocks separating portions of the columns, making this building very unique.

Devereaux walked up the sandstone stairs towards the door, and a brass plaque on the left side read "Mortimer House". Above the words was a gold lion's head. Devereaux went to open the front door; a massive solid wood door that towered over 2.5m in height and hung by huge brass hinges.

As he tried to turn the handle on the door, he found it fixed and unable to move. He looked to the left and saw a brass-framed doorbell.

He reached over and pressed the black button. Devereaux looked up, and to the right, a CCTV camera moved to focus on him. He looked back towards the door, and in a few seconds, it opened. He was greeted by a woman in her early 40s, brunette, attractive and wearing a body-hugging business skirt-suit with a sheer white blouse and a single string of Mikimoto pearls around her slender neck.

'Hello there, you must be John' she said. 'I'm Miranda Kershaw, manager of Mortimer House'.

'Good morning, Miranda' John replied.

Miranda led Devereaux across the reception hall to an ornate wooden door. She held a black plastic card in her right hand and swiped it against an innocent-looking wall near the doorframe. Secreted into the wall was an electronic scanner, invisible to the unacquainted. The faint sound of magnetic locks being unlocked was heard just before the door came ajar.

'Magnus is waiting for you in the library, down the hall on the left' Miranda said, as she looked straight into Devereaux's eyes and gave a teasing smile. Devereaux returned the gaze and allowing the corners of his mouth to edge upward in a subtle smile.

'John, welcome' Magnus said. 'Glad to see you home in one piece – and you did an outstanding job, I must say' he added.

'Sir, it's good to be home considering the circumstances' Devereaux said.

'Grab a seat' Magnus gestured to one of two Chesterfield leather chairs.

Devereaux remained standing and looked around the library. He walked over to the polished wooden shelf and saw a series of first editions.

He was looking at the spines of the books, and his index finger hooked the upper spine of a one and pulled it free from its rigid position on the shelf, supported by other first editions. He turned the book in the palm of his hands, his fingers splayed wide apart as to provide support for the book. "The Sun Also Rises" by Ernest Hemingway. Shit, a first edition on these shelves. Devereaux knew of this book being auctioned by Sotheby's for US$161,000.

Devereaux turned towards Magnus and asked, 'a first edition Hemingway?'

Magnus smiled and said, 'welcome to Mortimer House, John.'

Replacing the book on the shelf, Devereaux walked over to an antique Georgian sideboard and poured coffee, then walked back over and sat down in a single-seat Chesterfield.

'Connor, you're late' said Webb.

'Yes, terribly sorry sir, my tux didn't come back from the cleaners, terrible ordeal, really, I have to say… I must tell you about it sometime' Connor said with a defiant three-minute-late smile.

Devereaux was staring into his coffee, the sip he just took unintentionally spat back into the coffee cup as he fought back a laugh. Connor was a funny bastard, Devereaux thought. He was always able to summon a wisecrack or something to placate a tense moment. It had obviously worked as Webb had to turn away to avoid his smile being seen and losing his aloof composure.

'Please, take a seat' Webb casually directed Connor.

Webb remained standing and was silent for a few seconds as he thought about what he was to say.

'John, Operation Brimstone was a marvellous success' Webb said. 'UNTAC is on track, and we suspect that the near-to-mid term heroin imports into Australia will become a little scarcer – not halted by any means, of course, but certainly a decrease in capacity' he said.

'Thank you, sir, but we had the loss of two non-sanctioned individuals, not to mention one of them was a National Intelligence Agency (NIA), Intelligence officer, Captain Anchalee. I am sure that is going to cause a stir within the hornet's nest' Devereaux replied.

'Yes, that's true, John, but it was a necessary collateral expense we need to take on the chin' Connor replied.

'I agree, Connor' Webb added.

'However, it's something the service will be keeping a close eye on via our Bangkok Station and our friends at MI6. How are you feeling after the operation, John? I noticed you favouring your left leg?' Webb asked.

'A slight graze sir, nothing too exciting' Devereaux replied.

'Graze... from what?' Webb asked.

'Well, if I'm right, a 7.62mm x 39mm – most likely from an AK' Devereaux replied. 'But as I said, it's nothing. It's on the mend already' he added.

'John, our Bangkok Station is reporting that the Thai high command and the NIA are saying, as you suggested, that the hit was conducted by the Khmer. However, it has been reported that Maj. Getti said to the military police that he doubted it was a Khmer attack' Connor explained.

'We understand that Chatri was being groomed by his father to manage the NARCO trade that the General had built. You might also be interested to know that it is now assumed that Chatri and Anchalee were responsible for the murder of Steven Quinn, the Reuter's reporter slain in Patpong' Connor continued.

Webb opened a file, pulled out three photos and handed them over to Devereaux.

'These photos are from the Montien Hotel's security feeds on the night of Quinn's murder. From what we know from you and these photos, we are now sure that Anchalee did the hit on Quinn – working alongside her brother, Chatri' Webb said.

'And this photo was taken from a CCTV camera monitoring an intersection on Silom Road, not far from the Montien Hotel and around the time it is believed that Quinn was killed' he added.

'This could be anyone, two people on a motorcycle... in Bangkok... are you pulling the piss?' Devereaux asked.

Webb looked over at Connor.

'Look carefully at the photo. That motorcycle, John, is the same motorcycle that Major Chatri was on when you terminated the General in Aran' Connor interjected.

Devereaux looked more intently at the photo. 'You're right, it's the same bike' Devereaux agreed.

'They are a family of underworld figures, using positions of great privilege as a cover to acquire great wealth from illicit trades' Webb concluded.

'There is no doubt that "Operation Brimstone" debrided a substantive part of a cancer in the trade of Heroin.

CHAPTER 21

'Mantra-6'

SYDNEY

Webb walked over to where Devereaux had replaced the Hemmingway. He looked at the row of books, raised his right hand and extended his index finger, resting it on the spine of "The Sun Also Rises". He gently pushed the book in another 3mm to make sure it was perfectly aligned, his actions hinting at his OCD. Still looking at the bookshelf and surveying the books, he resumed speaking.

'It is my opinion, John, that the Service has slid into… let's say a "plateau of mediocrity". But I want to bring the Service back on the right track – at the very least, back on a far better trajectory than it has been in the past' Webb added with a hint of disdain.

'I'm tired of ASIS working with one arm tied behind its back, and I'm about to change all that. I want you to be part of it' Webb added with some authority. 'I have decided to implement a Deep Black programme by creating a new clandestine cell that will work on the fringe. The cell is to be codenamed "MANTRA-6."

Connor will head up the cell as the Director and we Webb paused, his eyes leaving the row of books and flickering over to Devereaux, 'we were hoping you would accept the role as Deputy Director.'

'Of course, this will require you to leave the military and work as a NOC, using "Mortimer House" as your cover.' 'This…' Webb, paused raising his hand in a circular motion, his eyes looking around the room, 'would be your office, essentially, as the President of "Mortimer Acquisitions", a small niche trading firm. That would be your cover.'

Connor added, 'to be honest, John, I couldn't think of anyone else I would rather have working next to me – and for once, we have an opportunity to make a real change.'

Devereaux sat back in his chair, his mind engaged in intense thought. 'Funding?' he asked.

'Funding has and will be looked after. Mortimer Acquisitions will have a starting budget of $50,000,000. That will be supplemented from your successful acquisitions and sales and added to as necessary with black funds. One stipulation – in order to create distance, your acquisitions must only be made offshore. Connor will provide you with the overall plan at a later date. Suffice it to say that your salary will be commensurate with the commercial sector and befitting the office which you hold. Are there any other questions?' Webb asked.

'Are there any fucking questions? Where do I start? How's this for size – what is the mission statement of MANTRA-6?' Devereaux asked impatiently.

'The mission of MANTRA-6, John, is to strengthen our foreign policy objectives through Clandestine Operations, particularly in the use of Violent, Deniable Covert Action' Webb responded with absolute conviction.

'Violent, Deniable Covert Action, John' Connor repeated Webb's words to ensure Devereaux understood.

Devereaux had, for years, lamented Australia's lame approach to any offensive strategic and tactical action. He saw Australia at the precipice of capitulation to a political correctness that had never been part of the Australian vocabulary. The very notion of taking a more offensive stance in the cold war, on fanatical religious freaks, or even taking a sledgehammer to the underworld was very appealing to him.

'So, the gloves are off?' Devereaux asked Webb looking over to Connor, then turned back at Devereaux, 'yes, John, the gloves are most definitely off, and you might say you are wearing a pair of brass knuckles just for good measure.'

Devereaux stood and walked around the room, contemplating everything that had been discussed, his mind in heavy thought and the room in absolute silence, his eyes scanning the spines of the rare leather-bound books.

'The "Violence" you speak of... such violence needs a special kind of man who is willing to unleash hell but in a controlled, disciplined manner. If I agree to take on this role, I want complete agreement that I choose my own team. I have the very "Hell Hounds" needed for such a role' Devereaux said, pausing and then turning to look at them both. 'That means you never tell me that someone else from the service is coming along for the ride or dictate to me how to achieve the objective' he added. 'If this is agreeable, then I'm in' Devereaux concluded.

Webb and Connor both stood, and the three men shook hands, sealing the agreement.

'Follow me, gentlemen' said Webb, leading them out of the library and down the corridor.

They walked down the passageway where they came to some heavy timber balustrading around a set of stairs that led down some four metres below their current level.

As they walked down the stairs, Devereaux noticed the red clay bricks and the brickwork made by master bricklayers.

The high brick vaulted ceilings extended the entire length of the corridor, which measured over thirty metres. Industrial lights overhead started to illuminate as sensors triggered their presence. Another passage led back the way they came directly under the level above. On either side of the corridor were heavy steel doors, all painted black.

'Cells?' Devereaux asked.

'Yes, John' replied Connor.

'This building used to be an old police station in the 1800's – we have repurposed the entire building to meet our new needs' he added.

As they walked along the corridor, Webb stopped at one door, made of heavy solid oak, with huge metal hinges – something you might see in a medieval castle.

'This has quite the gothic look to it, I'm surprised there are no Gargoyles guarding the entry.'

'You couldn't get a different decorator other than Herman Munster?' Devereaux added with a hint of sarcasm.

'Would you like Gargoyles, Dev?' Magnus asked with a subtle smirk.

Magnus Webb looked at Devereaux and said in a dry monotone, 'you are quite the master of rapid wit and repartee, aren't you?' Webb uttered, the corner of his mouth hinting a smile.

Now that's sarcasm at its finest, Devereaux thought.

Finally, a sense of humour from Webb. That's been a long time coming, thought Devereaux.

As the door opened, the lights turned on and illuminated an operations centre. Chart tables, computers, ceiling-mounted projectors, satellite communications systems… everything that one needs to run a sophisticated operation was present and accounted for.

'This is the heart of MANTRA-6' Webb stated with a sense of pride. 'Follow me' he added.

They left the Ops Room and went down the corridor to the room at the end. A sliding metal fire door was pulled back by Connor, on the inside, curtains of heavy rubber conveyer belt strips hung from the roof. Devereaux pushed his way past the heavy rubber curtains and was met by another wall. He turned to the left and walked past the wall and into a Killing House (KH).

They had constructed the KH so that they could train in secrecy for room combat activities inside buildings. It allowed them to construct any floor plan they needed and then practice doing room combat as though they were really in the target building. While smaller than what Devereaux was used to, it was outstanding – absolutely state of the art.

'This Close Quarter Battle (CQB) range is adequate, but has its limitations, as you can see. It will only allow for small calibre weapons – 9mm. So your Submachine Guns and pistols will be fine. For everything else, you will need to go off-reservation' Webb said. 'I know you chaps like your toys, so follow me.'

Walking out of the KH, they went to a room diagonally across on the right. The old cell door opened, and the lights illuminated a well-stocked armoury. Rows of weapons adorned the walls in racks. This included Heckler & Koch's family of Submachine Guns, M16/M203 Assault Rifles, AK-74 Assault Rifles, RPG's, Pistols and silenced or suppressed weapons and an assortment of edged weapons. Devereaux took an M16 off of the rack and looked over the weapon... no serial number! He replaced the weapon and randomly removed another – no serial number there, either.

'You won't find any serial numbers on any weapon here, Devereaux' Connor stated.

At the rear of the room, there was a caged area that was full of ammunition, grenades and an assortment of explosives.

As they left the room, Webb locked the door behind them, and as they walked along the corridor back to the stairwell, Webb pointed out a fully equipped gymnasium, two rooms to conduct training and planning, and a room full of Tatami mats for practising unarmed combat. The final room was located at the other end of the corridor. It was large and contained numerous types of doors and windows all attached to large metal frames that were on rollers so that they could be wheeled around the room. On the left side of the room, rows of locks were attached to frames, enabling operatives to practice their silent entry skills – picking locks and bypassing various alarm systems. There was much more to Mortimer House than first met the eye. It would prove to be the perfect headquarters for MANTRA-6.

Back in the library, and standing near the Chesterfield sofas, Webb said, 'Connor and Miranda will show you to your office and the rest of the Mortimer Acquisitions elements of the building. On your way-out John, see Miranda – she will organise and take you to a tailor to get a new wardrobe. Your suit looks highly unbecoming of the President of Mortimer Acquisitions' Webb said with raised eyebrows.

'Miranda will also take you to your new apartment here in Sydney – walking distance from here, in fact, ol' boy.'

'I don't need to remind you, Dev, but what we are about to embark on is highly illegal, but highly necessary.' Webb paused and looked down to the carpet underfoot and raised his head slowly to meet the eyes of both Connor and Devereaux.

'Gentlemen, we start today' Webb added with a dignified tone.

CHAPTER 22

'Cross-Deck'

MEDITERRANEAN

March 1993

02:31hrs

The Corsican man at the helm steered the trawler through the gentle Mediterranean Sea. The boat, the "Prince de la Mer", had been trawling the Spinola Spur for sardines for some 64 nautical miles (NM) off the coast of Nice.

'Captain, bearing Two-Seven-Zero degrees, at 10 knots, Sir' said the Corsican. The Captain looked over at the tall Russian and said, 'Aleksandr, we are in position and on course for the intercept in 7 minutes - off the port side.'

Aleksandr Drozdov turned and looked at the radar, the vector for intercept matching the steady blip on the radar screen, their target tracking 270° at 5 knots.

Drozdov picked up the microphone, 'Prepare the boom and winch for haulage – portside. Hook up the cargo for transfer and maintain light discipline' he blustered in guttural Russian, the crew responding instantly by attaching the cargo hook to the cargo net. The cargo was four olive drab coloured wooden crates, marked in yellow-stencilled writing, "9K32 Strela-2:

Qty-4" (SA-7 GRAIL) The Russian made surface to air, shoulder-launched missiles capable of taking out aircraft to 3,700m.

The 16 missiles could evoke utter chaos in the wrong hands.

'There she is, just left of the bow, 200 metres' said the Corsican.

Drozdov and the Captain moved forward to the bridge windows and looked intently at the black silhouette as they closed the distance.

'Bring the boat alongside and match her speed – no more than 3 metres apart, and hold course', the Captain said with authority.

'Yes, Captain' the Corsican replied.

Drozdov walked out on to the deck and braced himself against the railing, pulling out a torch with a red filter over the lens and sending the letter "R" in Morse code.

The black silhouette replied with a green "K".

'Alright, pull alongside but match and maintain speed and heading' Drozdov ordered.

The Captain, looking at the Corsican, said, 'Make it so."

'Yes, Captain' came the acknowledgement from the Corsican.

The two black silhouettes came alongside each other. Drozdov ordered the deck crew to manoeuvre the boom out over the port side and across to the deck of the other trawler.

The boom lifted the cargo off of the deck of the Prince de la Mer. As the deck crew steadied it, the boom operator started to swing the cargo across the gap between the two vessels. As the boom was in position above the deck of the other trawler, Drozdov lowered his hand, indicating to the boom operator to lower the cargo. The boom operator pushed the lever forward, lowering the missiles onto the other boat's deck.

The crew on the other vessel scurried around unhooking the cargo and moving the hook over to another waiting cargo net, which was filled with a wooden pine crate.

The deckhand took hold of the heavy iron hook and snapped it on to the cargo net and pushed forward the safety bar to the closed position. A single green flash of light emitted from the lead deck hand's torch, indicating to commence lifting the cargo. Once the cargo was 3m above the deck, the boat, now free from its load, steered to port and steamed off into the darkness, it's task now complete.

'Commence haulage back onto the deck' yelled the Captain over the microphone.

The boom operator manoeuvred the boom back across the deck of the Prince de la Mer, and the cargo was lowered onto the deck and secured. Drozdov walked impatiently across the deck and unsecured the hook from the net, ordering the pine box to be removed from the open deck and secured below.

'Set course for Port de Plaisance at Beaulieu–Sur–Mer, 12kts' bellowed the Captain.

'Yes, Captain - set course for Port de Plaisance at Beaulieu–Sur–Mer, 12kts' replied the Corsican.

The vessel had been sailing for thirty minutes since the rendezvous and cross deck transfer.

'Captain, running lights, sir?' asked the Corsican.

'Roger, activate running lights' said the Captain.

The Prince de la Mer was set on course for Port de Plaisance, a small marina five kilometres east of Nice.

311

Drozdov was below preparing the cargo, transferring the contents of the pine crate into waterproof valises for ease of handling on debarkation. 500 individually wrapped packages in aluminium foil; a white plastic sticker on each package and in the centre of the white label, a Red Thai Naga embossed each package of heroin.

It was 04:20hrs and the sky started to show a hint that the dawn was approaching. The Prince de la Mer edged her bow into its pen at the marina while the crew hastily secured the bow and stern lines to the concrete jetty and commenced unloading its sardine catch from the Spinola Spur. The white foam boxes were brought up from the freezer in the vessel's hull below, while above, a small conveyer belt system moved the foam boxes of fresh sardines across the deck and onto the dock.

Drozdov stood in the shadows on the upper deck, using binoculars to scan the port for any sign of surveillance efforts before raising his hand, gesturing to the driver of a white Renault Commercial Van that it was safe to approach the boat.

The driver of the van reversed the vehicle along the dock towards the boat. Once the van was in position, and with Drozdov still maintaining overwatch, he signalled the crew to bring up the cargo. The crew quickly retrieved the valises from the deck below and transferred them into the van and closed the door.

Drozdov entered the bridge on the vessel and placed a grey plastic bag on the navigation chart table – the bag contained US$100,000.

'Thank you again, Captain Legrand. See you next time' Drozdov stretched his arm out to meet Christophe Legend's already outstretched hand before he turned and left the vessel.

Drozdov walked along the boardwalk to a waiting black 7 Series BMW. He opened the door and slid into the back seat. A man holding two tumblers of vodka passed one to Drozdov, his forearm heavily scarred from burns.

'Welcome back Aleksandr, I trust the transfer all went to plan.'

'The operation went like clockwork' Drozdov muttered in reply. 'This is the first shipment of 500kg of 99% pure heroin. The next delivery will be ready in a month from now.

This is just the start of a very prosperous business venture together' Chatri said as he raised his vodka in a toast... 'Nah-Zda-Rovh-yeh' cheers, he said in Russian.

YOU HAVE TO LIVE IT AND SURVIVE IT
TO WRITE IT!

NEVER MISS A BEAT
ON ALL THE LATEST NEWS FROM

RUSSEL
HUTCHINGS
&
MANTRA-6

BE THE FIRST TO FIND OUT ABOUT NEW RELEASES
AND EVENTS WITH RUSSEL

REGISTER AS A VIP READER...

www.mantra-6.com